BRING ON FOREVER

by

LETA BLAKE

An Original Publication from Leta Blake Books, first published as Halsey Harlow via Lucky Honey Books in 2018
Written and published by Leta Blake
Cover by Dar Albert
Formatted by BB eBooks

First Edition, 2018
Second Edition, 2021

ISBN: 979-8-88841-071-4

Their age difference tore them apart. Can a chance encounter bring them together?

Advertising hotshot Grey Blackburn never expected a second chance with Blaine Kellerman. Ten years ago, their age difference tore them apart when Blaine left Nashville to pursue his dreams in filmmaking. But when they meet again in New York City at a swanky party for one of Grey's best clients, all bets are off.

The explosive attraction between them hasn't changed in their years apart, but their lives certainly have. Grey's an absent uncle to a teenage boy who is suddenly bursting with a strong need for his attention, and Blaine has his own unique domestic situation that is rife with potential problems.

Drawn together again, their fresh start must survive hurting other people and their own terrible insecurities. Can they really leave the past behind to build a bright future?

This book is 40,000 words of a second chance love story complete with a happy ending!

CHAPTER ONE

THE PARTY WAS going full tilt when Grey arrived.

Versace-clad women danced arm-in-arm with Armani-suited men, lips pressed against cheeks in greeting, and all around the room handsome, elegant men held Grey's eyes just a little too long in open invitation.

Grey leaned against the well-stocked bar and motioned for another drink, congratulating himself on making enough good choices in life to land him here. The decision, made four years ago, to open a sister agency in New York, leaving his former underlings in charge of his advertising shop in Nashville, had been a wise one. That bold stroke had resulted in multi-billion dollar accounts, a summer home in Italy, and more money than he thought it prudent to spend in his lifetime. Although, beyond a nice bundle set aside for the future benefit of his teenage nephew, Reed, Grey fully intended to see if he *could* spend the majority of it, before expiring on a tropical beach surrounded by hot, naked, young men.

Leaning against an exquisitely papered wall, he sipped his Jim Beam, letting it heat his tongue. The strong scent rolled through his sinuses before he swallowed, and the burn chased the liquid down to his stomach. The penthouse was extravagantly decorated with leather and wood furniture touched by silver and gold accents. The place spun Grey's head even on a normal night, without the celebrity-level, giant floral arrangements that now filled the room with a buzzy scent. Waiters in black tie circled with drinks, appetizers, and tiny little desserts that were as pretty as they were delicious.

Grey kept his head high, reminding himself that he deserved to be here as much as anyone else, and banished the little voice inside that wondered what a loser from Nashville had to offer the Big Apple's upper-crust. He'd come by his invitation honestly. The party was part of the launch of a new line of evening bags by one of his favorite accounts, Johansson Handbags.

Dominique Johansson, designer of the stylish handbags currently clutched in the hands of the brightest starlets and most beautiful heiresses worldwide, had insisted Grey attend tonight. She'd batted her glittery lashes at him, flipped her long, snow white hair over her shoulder, and assured him that he'd meet many prospective new clients, all of whom would literally beg to be added to his roster.

It wasn't as though he'd really needed the coaxing, though. Grey never missed one of Dominique's soirees if he could prevent it. He'd scored his best hook-ups in recent memory through Dominique's connections. He had no doubt that he'd get laid tonight, and well laid at that. The key was in picking the right man, and, as always, there were plenty to choose from.

The dark-eyed Romeo in the corner who'd been eyeing him flirtatiously held promise. His lips were lush, his hands large, and his package was nicely emphasized by his form-fitting pants. But the redhead leaning against the opposite end of the bar had also piqued Grey's interest by demonstrating dexterity with his tongue. He'd used it to tie a cherry stem for Dominique's entertainment a few moments prior. And, based on the strong hand gripping his forearm, he now had another opportunity with Dominique's assistant, Johan, a slightly older, Scandinavian-born, hottie with an ass to die for.

"Dominique mentioned earlier that there's a young man here she wants you to meet. A gentleman named Mark Vanderhalder."

Johan, using only the pressure from his hand in a practiced way, turned Grey's attention toward a beautiful, late-twenties, strawberry-blond man standing in front of the couch laughing amongst a group of friends. His nose was a bit long, but otherwise Grey had no complaints. This Mark Vanderhalder looked delicate and like his skin would pink up nicely when he got excited.

Grey smirked, already making plans for seduction.

Johan went on, "He's not the owner, but he's got clout. Serious clout. And he's in a good position within the firm to bring you straight to the decision-maker if he likes you."

Grey smiled, licked his lips and murmured, "Oh, he'll like me all right. Thank you, Johan. And to think I was going to take *you* home. I guess you lose yet again."

Johan laughed, gripped Grey's arm firmly, and indicated Mark Vanderhalder again. "Sorry, but you won't be taking Vanderhalder home either. He's in a *relationship*."

Grey sipped his drink and fought his amusement. He'd have the guy bent over Dominique's fabulous guest bathroom sink taking his dick within the hour.

"With the decision-maker—" Johan added and gestured with his drink as the crowd in front of the couch parted, affording Grey a view of the individual holding court there. "And there he is, Dominique's latest pet, the CEO of the top animation production company outside of Disney-fucking-Studios."

Grey sipped his drink again to cover any stray show of emotion that the blond hair, smirking red lips, and piercing blue eyes staring straight at him might have engendered.

"His name's Blaine Kellerman," Johan continued. "I'm sure you've heard of him."

Grey snorted. "You could say that."

"He owns Chill Blaine Enterprises," Johan continued, "He's only the biggest name in gay Hollywood since Neil Patrick what's-his-face—"

Grey held Blaine's gaze, allowing a small, warm smile to grace his lips, hoping it covered the turmoil that'd sparked inside him upon seeing the only man he'd ever let himself truly love.

Inappropriate as that love had been when Blaine was only just eighteen and Grey a young ad exec a year away from turning thirty, it was still the only real love he'd ever known. He'd never blamed Blaine for leaving when his big break came along. He'd been just a kid, ten years younger than Grey, so of course he'd sprouted wings and flown.

Never mind that Grey's heart had never recovered.

Blaine broke the long-held eye contact, glancing up at his still-talking partner and wrinkling his nose at whatever Mark Vanderhalder was holding forth about. Pushing up from the sofa, Blaine gestured with his glass toward the bar, and then headed straight toward Grey.

Johan's fingers gripped Grey's arm painfully. "Don't look now, but he's coming over here—"

"Grey." Blaine's voice was warm, deep, and shiver-inducing. The smug expression on his face let Grey know that he wasn't all that surprised to find his ex-lover here. "How are you?"

Johan garbled something beside him, then spit out, "Mr. Kellerman, this is Mr. Grey Blackburn—"

"No need for introductions, Johan," Blaine said. "We know each other well."

"Knew," Grey corrected, needlessly, and regretted it as soon as it was out of his mouth.

Johan made his excuses with frayed apologies that made little sense. Grey wasn't sure why the normally sedate man had become so frazzled. He shook his head in confusion as Johan darted across the room.

Blaine laughed, his brow raised sardonically. "People treat me that way now. It's strange because inside I feel the same—you know, just your Doll Face from Music City—but apparently I'm not the same at all."

"I'd say not." No, now Blaine was a big fucking success.

Blaine broke into his signature grin. It made Grey's heart stand still. "Now, I'm *Blaine Kellerman, producer,* and that makes people behave like insane little rats."

Grey decided not to comment on the analogy. He felt twitchy enough inside to suspect that if he wasn't careful, Blaine would chalk him up as another rodent worthy of his disdain. A mix of emotions played inside of him as the silence lingered. Eventually, after another swallow of Beam, he simply said, "You look the same."

"A little older. A little fatter."

Grey smiled. It was true that Blaine wasn't as lithe as he'd been ten years ago, but he was no less handsome. "Yeah, well, who am I to talk, right? I'm almost forty years old now."

"You're forty-three!" Blaine laughed, blue eyes twinkling in delight.

"All right, then. Forty-three."

"No grays in that dark hair of yours and, let me guess, Botox is to thank for keeping those pretty hazel eyes crow's feet free?"

Grey smirked. "My plastic surgeon tells me I have the forehead of an eighteen year old."

Blaine laughed again, his grin lighting up a dark spot in

Grey's hardened heart. Then Blaine sobered. He wiped a hand over his upper lip and sighed, shoulders dropping. "Seriously, you look great. You always look great."

Grey choked back sarcasm, his usual response to compliments, and instead said earnestly, "So do you."

Blaine leaned against the bar staring with so much intensity that Grey *felt* the warmth. His heart clenched in anticipation of hurt, his chest opened up with a wild, vibrant hope that he'd tried to bury, and his cock thickened with the hot desire that Blaine had never failed to inspire in him.

Grey took a gulp of his whiskey and forced a nonchalant study of the other party guests, before turning his gaze out the wide windows lining the penthouse toward the blinking lights of the city. He looked anywhere but Blaine's eyes. He sucked in a long, soothing breath, and tried to chill the burn under his skin, angry with himself for his body's betrayal. He was supposed to have put this all behind him, far in the past with all the other dead things he'd once cared about, like his father, his innocence, and definitely romantic love.

"Dominique has been talking you up to Mark," Blaine said, nodding his head toward his still-chatting lover who had now been joined by the hostess herself. She laughed at whatever Mark said and flipped her hair over her shoulder.

"Has she?"

"She wants him to convince me to use you for Chill Blaine's next marketing initiative."

So, Blaine had known that Grey was living in New York and had possibly even expected that he'd be at the party. Was this the reason Dominique had been so insistent that he attend? Grey swallowed his rolling emotions and asked, "And what did you tell Mark?"

"I told him that I trust his judgment. I didn't tell him about us, though." Blaine caught his gaze then and held it. "Too much history, and I didn't want to get into it."

Grey nodded. He understood Blaine's unspoken request that he not bring up their prior relationship to his current lover.

"So, I guess I'll leave it up to Mark to contact you about the campaign. I'm not sure just how involved I'll be in it all. I generally leave those things up to Mark, preferring to focus on the production of creative content." He loosed a slow smile. "But I'd love to catch up with you while I'm in town. It's been a long time."

"Isn't that what we just did?" Grey bit down on his tongue. If he could retract that last comment, he would. Turning his eyes to rush over the room, he noticed that the dark-eyed Romeo in the corner was still offering, and Grey lifted his drink in a return gesture out of habit.

"Well, it appears the lion has caught his prey for the evening." Blaine pushed away from the bar. "I suppose I'll get back to Mark now."

Grey muttered, "Yes, mustn't keep the husband waiting."

Blaine smiled, his eyes glittering smartly. "We aren't married. I don't tie myself to one man. I fuck who I want, when I want, and Mark knows it."

Grey swallowed hard, remembering when he'd rejected Blaine's young pleas for monogamy, declaring them heteronormative and unrealistic. When really, he'd just been afraid. "Good to know some lessons stuck."

"Oh, a lot of lessons stuck." Blaine's old hurt shimmered in his eyes for a moment.

Grey's stomach twisted. "I don't care about the details of your relationship," he protested. "Why are you telling me?"

"Because I've always wanted you to be proud of me, Grey." Blaine cocked his head, growing deadly serious. "Didn't you know that?"

Grey watched as Blaine turned his back and walked away, never once glancing back to see Grey's reaction.

It hurt just like it had the first time.

CHAPTER TWO

"**T**EN YEARS IS a long time." Grey repeated those words to himself again and again. The dark-eyed Romeo had been satisfactory, but ultimately boring, and had already been given the boot hours earlier. "A lot can change in ten years."

Grey studied himself in his bathroom mirror, the black and silver of the tiles and fixtures glinting all around him. No matter what Blaine said, he *did* look older, a little grayer, and a tad more wrinkled. The hair transplants had covered the balding issue to a large degree, but thinness was still visible on top. However, his stomach was still ripped, and his thighs strong—even so, he'd definitely lost his youth. He was solidly a *man* now, with none of the little boy that he used to sometimes see in his own face even into his thirties.

"A lot can change."

But inside he felt the same. He still liked to party and fuck. He still liked to watch cartoons on the sly, and play video games over the internet with his nephew Reed, and, despite his sister Fawn's confusion about it, he was still the hero of their younger brother, Jamie. Of their whole queer family, he was the only one who'd had the balls to come out to their dearly departed father after all, and he'd taken the beatings for it. Jamie had told him much later in life that while it'd been scary, he'd thought Grey was brave at the time.

For her part, Fawn had kept her bisexuality to herself until Pa had died, and Reed, her illegitimate son from a college hookup, had been the ultimate cover. Jamie, so much younger, hadn't come out to anyone in the family, though his queerness had been obvious to Grey for years, until he'd hooked up with his Belmont University professor, now husband, Caldwell Lovell, his senior year in college. Working out his daddy issues, no doubt, in the wake of their father's death.

But while Jamie looked up to Grey, declaring him "the ultimate successful queer", he'd gone a completely different way in his own life, choosing to settle down with his professor and live the heteronormative dream. Grey often wished Jamie would come live in New York, but deep down he knew Jamie would never leave Nashville. It was his home. Not to mention, it served as the base of operations for Jamie and Caldwell's family—which was ever changing and growing as he and Caldwell fostered more and more children.

Like, an endless stream of children.

In Nashville Jamie could stay close to Fawn's family and their mother, too, of course. And then there was Emma, their first foster baby, who was only eleven. Jamie wanted to stay close to her and to the mother she'd been returned to. They'd bonded deeply during that first fostering experience, and Jamie and Caldwell continued to play the role of father in the little girl's life.

Brushing his damp hair, Grey's thoughts turned to Reed, his nephew, and his own promise to be a father to the boy. Sometimes he thought Jeanine, Fawn's butch young lover of the last four years, was a better masculine role model than he could ever be. But by the time Jeanine had shown up on the scene, Reed was already a pre-teen, and hadn't been interested in playing happy family with two mothers. Fawn continued to ask him to spend more time with Reed. Especially lately.

Guilt clawed at his gut and he shoved it down. He'd been busy lately, that was all, and the kid didn't really need someone like him anyway. He deserved a better pseudo-dad. Like Jamie or Caldwell. He should talk to them about taking over the job.

When Fawn and Jeanine had decided to have another child together, this one carried by Jeanine, he'd thanked the heavens above that they hadn't asked him for a donation. Instead, they'd found a donor from Vanderbilt Medical School, and he'd heard a rumor from their mother that Jamie and Caldwell had declared themselves up for the father role, so adding Reed to their duties wouldn't be hard. Which would be a blessing all around for everyone, Grey was sure.

Speaking of, Jeanine's kid was probably due any day now.

He really should call Fawn soon. And Reed, too, of course.

"Some things never change," Grey said. Like how he much he failed at this surrogate fatherhood thing. Like how much he loved his siblings even though he sucked at showing it. Like how he still felt about Blaine.

God, Blaine.

Even now Grey didn't know how to explain the way their relationship had started. He'd first spotted Blaine at the club Tribe in Nashville, dancing his youthful heart out under the disco ball and flashing lights. Drawn in by Blaine's beauty and light, the delicious way he moved, and the joy in his carefree face, Grey—panicked at facing his upcoming thirtieth birthday—hadn't been able to resist a taste.

But what should have been a backroom blowjob for kicks had turned into so much more. The annoying brat with a shattering grin kept coming around and somehow managed to worm his way into Grey's heart. And, for four beautiful and miserable years, Blaine had refused to go.

Grey wondered even now how much more he might have accomplished in his life, what a better person he might have been, if Blaine had stuck around for good, if Grey had been the kind of man that Blaine would have stuck around for. Or, if he wanted to be brutally honest with himself, if *he'd* been the kind of man who'd have put Blaine first, pulled up stakes, and gone with him the time came to take his chance.

Glaring at himself in the mirror, he went on admitting hard truths to himself.

The truth was Grey had lost Blaine twice. The first time was little by little, as Grey's bitterness and refusal to change had robbed them both of the youthful joy that had once been Blaine's greatest gift. The second time was when Blaine came to his senses and took his life back, along with a plane to Los Angeles. Years of delayed pain were finally resolved with the finality of Grey's old apartment door slamming shut, leaving nothing of Blaine behind but a lingering scent in the pillows.

That had faded over time.

Grey's regret had not.

Jamie once told him that he hadn't been sure Grey would survive the loss. Fawn had said she'd feared for his sanity. But he'd gutted it out, refusing to give in to his desire to crawl across the country on his hands and knees to beg Blaine for forgiveness.

To declare his undying love.

To confess that he was scared of monogamy, and commitment, terrified of trusting any man, even one younger than him, with his heart.

To tell the truth about the brutality of his father's beatings, of his horrible first fuck with an older man that'd stolen his virginity in a perversion of power.

To speak of all his darkness, and take the biggest risk of all:

beg for Blaine to love him anyway.

In the end, he'd choked those urges down. He'd picked up the pieces of his truncated life and moved on, telling himself that he was stronger than ever for having survived a broken heart. Even one mostly self-inflicted.

"A lot can change in ten years," he said again.

Blaine hadn't, though. Despite the extra pounds and the start of some wrinkles. He'd still been his wry, challenging, intelligent self. And he'd looked amazing at the party, smartly dressed and shining as bright as ever.

But Grey wasn't surprised by that.

He'd seen the photos in the magazines, keeping an eye on his protégé, his young ex-lover, and he'd been so proud that Blaine had become a fabulous, fucking success. Bedding gorgeous men all over the world, and learning to smile an approximation of the old grin that had been stolen from him during the lengthy sadness of his all-wrong relationship with Grey in Nashville.

Blaine might not be as lean as he once was, but his maturity suited him well. It brought out an almost rugged sexuality that offset his somewhat too-pretty good looks. Grey wondered if his skin tasted the same, if he still groaned in that soft, halting way when he was about to come.

Grey's reflection looked skeptical as he intoned, "Ten years is a long time."

To be in love with someone that he'd never have again. And yet, apparently not long enough for the hurt and longing to go away.

Grey had felt the heat between them tonight and he knew Blaine had, too. The sexy blink that Blaine had basically patented had been turned on him from the beginning of their conversation, and the way Blaine's body had angled his way, the small tells that hid in the set of Blaine's lips, the tone of Blaine's voice, all declared that he still wanted Grey, too.

But a 'long time, no see' fuck wasn't on Grey's to-do list for the week. Or for his lifetime. Not when it came to Blaine.

Mainly because Grey knew there'd be no way to stop his heart from breaking again when Blaine left. That was inevitable.

Or was it? Grey looked at his reflection for a long time. What would Blaine see in him now? A sexy, wealthy, intelligent man? Or—

"Ten years is a long time but some things never change. I still look fucking hot," Grey muttered, before turning his back on the mirror and heading to bed.

CHAPTER THREE

MARK VANDERHALDER WAS on Grey's extension at nine-oh-two the following Monday morning. He had a pleasant voice, was obviously clever, and spoke of Blaine as 'my partner' with a tone that made it plain that he was definitely way more than Blaine's business partner.

"Blaine has a vision for his company, Mr. Blackburn. He's usually a very hands-on leader. And, frankly, based on Dominique's recommendation, as well as what I know personally of Blackburn Advertising's work, I think your firm's advice might be of interest to him. We look forward to hearing any suggestions you have for our company's upcoming marketing initiative. My partner wants to increase profitability this upcoming year, and I don't want to let him down."

"I assure you, Blaine Kellerman won't be let down. Blackburn Advertising will see to that."

Grey found himself cataloguing any perceived weakness that he could find in Mark, small things like the timbre of his voice and the subtle tick in his throat when he inhaled. But it wasn't until they disconnected the call and he found himself muttering, "Enjoy him while you can, Mark," that he realized he'd decided to win Blaine back—for good this time.

Grey asked his assistant, Amelia, to schedule an appointment for the initial pitch and for Mark to drop by to tour Blackburn Advertising. He'd found that showing his clients around his unique and spacious office in Chelsea gave them a preview of what to expect from Blackburn Advertising as an agency, as well as impressing them with their modern, daring venue.

When his phone rang at three o'clock, Grey knew before he even looked at the caller ID that it was Jamie. His younger brother had always possessed a kind of sixth sense when it came to Grey's emotional state.

Grey answered his phone, saying, "Hey, Jamie. What's up?"

"The youngest kid is still shitting in his pants, the oldest is suspended from school, and I'm supposed to meet with the middle kid's teacher tomorrow. But, in better news, Emma is going to be the lead in the school play. Oh, and, you should probably know that Jeanine has been put on restriction due to pre-term labor again, and Reed—you know, your nephew? the one you promised to be there for?—told me that he's planning to come see you in New York for a week whether you invite him up there or not."

"Sounds like an eventful day."

"You could say that. What's new with you?"

Grey chose to ignore the comments about Reed and leaned back in his chair, playing with his pencil. "I didn't catch his name. He was pretty hot, I guess. A little too…pretty. Big eyes, big lips. Kind of effeminate. But he sucked cock like a pro."

"Well, when you've fucked everyone on earth, I guess your standards get pretty fucking high. Or should I say low?" Jamie snarked.

"And I saw Blaine," Grey said, keeping his tone even.

Jamie went silent for a long moment. Grey could just imagine his dark brown eyes going even darker, and his long fingers ripping anxiously through his curly, salt-and-pepper hair. "Mama talked to him a few days ago. They keep up, remember?"

"Yeah." His mother had loved Blaine more than she'd probably ever loved Grey. When they'd broken up, she'd taken it almost as poorly as Grey had himself. Until she figured out that she didn't have to lose Blaine just because Grey had.

It was strange, though, that she kept her conversations with him mostly to herself. She was a blabbermouth about nearly everything else, which was one reason why Grey avoided calling her whenever he could.

"So, yeah. I knew he was in New York," Jamie said. "I guess I hoped you wouldn't find out." There was another long pause. "How'd you run into him? In a backroom or something?"

"Nope. A client's party."

Jamie sighed. "Did you fuck him?"

"No, I didn't fuck him!" Grey scoffed. He paused and added as innocently as possible, "Besides, he's in a relationship."

"Wait a minute, I know that tone, Grey!" Jamie's voice grew high-pitched, on the verge of a drama-queen moment. "Don't do this to yourself. Let it go."

"I don't know what you're talking about, Jamie. Besides, I can't let it go—"

"Yes, you can. And you will."

"He's going to be my client. His *partner* wants me to pitch for the company. Apparently, the reviews from my current accounts have him all atwitter to get Blackburn Advertising to do their next campaign."

"Grey…" Jamie's voice held warning. "What are you planning?"

"Nothing. I mean, the partner seems pretty secure. I'm sure a little competition won't shake him up too badly."

"You should walk away." Jamie sighed heavily, and Grey continued to twirl his pencil. Inside, he knew Jamie was right.

"It's been how long? Ten years or some shit like that? Is it really so important to your giant fucking ego to ruin his relationship, just to prove that he still wants you? You're Grey fucking Blackburn! Of course he still wants you!"

Grey was silent. Jamie was wrong. It wasn't about his ego. Finally, he said, "It's not like that, Jamie."

Jamie remained quiet for just a moment, and then Grey could hear a barrage of kids' voices in the background. "Hold on. Let me deal with this. Don't eat that!" Jamie yelled. "That's for Caldwell's dinner. And go up to your room." Then the voices argued, yelled, screeched, and dissipated. Jamie huffed back onto the line. "Grey, you don't even know him any more. What if he's changed?"

"He hasn't changed."

"You can't—"

"Listen, Jamie, I've got to go. Have fun with the little pants-shitter and all the rest. Get the date of Emma's play to Amelia so that her Uncle Grey can send roses on opening night. I was always her favorite foster-uncle, you know."

"Grey—"

"And let me know when Jeanine pops that kid out. I'd like to send a card at least. Later, Jamie."

The dial tone was a relief. He didn't need Jamie voicing all of his innermost fears. They whispered to him loudly enough every time he remembered Blaine's eyes and lips and voice—and that was approximately every other second.

Still it'd been ten years and he was old enough to admit he'd been an idiot to let Blaine go. He wasn't going to lose him twice, no matter what it cost him.

CHAPTER FOUR

L ESS THAN A week before the initial pitch, Grey was methodical-
ly studying up on Blaine's company. He knew the idea for the
campaign had to be nothing less than brilliant. There could be no
room for error or miscalculation. Chill Blaine's initial campaign
might not be his biggest account, but it could end up being his
most important one.

His first move was to contact Dominique Johansson and,
after polite greetings (if one could call discussion of their
respective prior night's sexual escapades 'polite'), he asked her as
carefully as possible, "What do you know about Blaine Kellerman?"

"Liked him, did you, love? I saw you talking to him at the
bar. You do realize that he's very taken, don't you?"

"Why Dominique, is everything about sex when it comes to
you?" He smiled as her laughter pealed over the line. "I'm merely
asking because his partner is apparently besotted with me due to
your rave reviews and, probably, the rumors of my prowess in
bed, too. I just wonder if I need to fear Mr. Kellerman's shotgun
for stealing his lover."

Dominique laughed some more, and then said, "Oh, even if
that were true, which I know it isn't because Mark is obsessed,
obsessed, with Blaine, you wouldn't need to fear for your life.
They have a very open relationship. Very, very open. Well, on
Blaine's end of things—or so I understand."

Grey stuck his tongue in his cheek and hummed thoughtfully. So, Blaine hadn't been lying about not being Mr. Monogamy after all. "How long have they been together?"

"Oh, about two years, off and on. Mostly off, to be honest. Blaine has made it quite clear that Mark is not the end-all and be-all of his existence. Sadly, I can't say the same for Mark."

"So," Grey tried to turn the discussion back to business on some level before Dominique became too suspicious of his questions. "I suppose that appealing to Mr. Vanderhalder's desires to be associated with Blackburn Advertising will not make all that much of an impression on Mr. Kellerman with regards to consideration of our campaign."

Dominique chirped in amusement. "Oh, no, dearest. No, no, no. Blaine gives Mark nearly every whim his heart desires, so long as it fits into the scheme of Blaine's vision for the company. They have a very…symbiotic relationship. A very healthy one in many ways," she clucked in thought. "Although, sometimes, it's my opinion that Blaine gets bored. He seems to like a little drama in his life."

"I see. And, hey, thank you for the referrals. You keep sending them my way like this and I might have to break down and give you what you want."

"Oh, my love, you know that it isn't Mark that is besotted with you, but I—your very own Dominique—who would ride you until you couldn't be ridden any more!"

Grey laughed. "Well, that wouldn't be very long, considering your lady parts would make my dick shrivel up and fall off."

"Dirty boy! Dirty, dirty boy! Talk dirty to me some more!"

When Grey hung up the phone, he leaned back in his chair again listening to the echoing silence in the office. Everyone else had long since gone home, and he pondered the shadows on the ceiling. He was tired of feeling like he'd never stop missing someone, tired of that gaping spot in his chest that he could feel when he let himself grow quiet. He thought about calling Fawn; she had always been one of the few who really understood how he felt about Blaine, and had treated him with gentleness after he'd lost Blaine's love. She'd told him that he deserved to love and to be loved in return. He'd cried in her arms while she stroked his hair.

There was a time when he hadn't believed her on that front, but he was older now, and wiser. And the truth was that no one deserved the kind of love that Blaine had once given him, back when he'd been young and naïve, before Grey had ruined it, but he wanted it anyway. And he'd have it, because he was, like Jamie said, Grey fucking Blackburn.

CHAPTER FIVE

"**A**NOTHER WAREHOUSE, HUH? Well, never let anyone say that you're inconsistent, Grey."

The layouts for Chill Blaine Enterprises were splayed over his desk, and his eyes were blurred from trying to figure out just what exactly was wrong with the second image—should he reverse it? Make it black and white? He was utterly unprepared.

"Blaine," Grey leaned back in his chair and let instinct take over. "I wasn't expecting you."

"I told—Amelia? Is that her name?"

Grey nodded.

"I told her you wouldn't mind me not being announced. I have no doubt, though, that she's currently pissing in her panties thinking that you're going to go out there and carve her a new one for letting me in without warning." Blaine smiled provocatively, eyelids slightly lowered, blink in full flirt-mode. "Are you?"

"No. I'm going to fire her."

Blaine grinned. "Oh, you were always so sexy when you got tough with your employees. Can I watch?"

Grey chuckled, and said, "Is there something I can help you with?"

"I just wanted to see who, or rather what, I might be getting into bed with here. Chill Blaine Enterprises is my baby, you know. I'm rather protective of it and I like to do my research."

Grey smirked. "According to my calendar there are several

more days before our appointment, and your partner is supposed to tour the agency tomorrow."

"I think surprise visits are much more revealing." Blaine stepped up to the edge of the desk, leaned against it and finished in a husky voice, "Don't you?"

Grey turned back to the spreads on his desk. "I'm working on your campaign right now." He indicated the second board. "There's something wrong with the image here. Do you think it needs to be reversed?"

Blaine sat on the edge of the desk and leaned over. "Hmm, not reversed, just more to the left."

Grey nodded and made a note. His palms were sweaty, and when he stood up, he casually ran his hands down his pants legs. Then he clapped them together. "Well, then, shall we do the tour?"

"Grey?"

"Yes?" Grey looked into Blaine's eyes and felt as though he'd been pulled into the sea. He couldn't look away, and yet he knew his face revealed too much.

"Are you seeing anyone?"

Grey snorted, crossed his arms over his chest, and leaned back on his heels. "Not very subtle, Blaine."

"I'm not into subtle. Who has time for that anymore? So, tell me…is there anyone that you fuck more than once?"

Grey scratched his chin, trying to play down the fact that his heart was beating double-time in his chest. Horribly dangerous hope soared through him again. "Hmm, more than once, yes. But rarely more than twice, and never more than five times." He sighed dramatically. "They tend to bore me after that."

"We must've fucked thousands of times," Blaine whispered.

Grey lowered his eyes. Heat rose inside of him as he looked

back up to Blaine's intense blue gaze. "You have a partner."

"I'm not into monogamy. I fuck who I want—"

"I know the lines, Blaine. I made them up." Grey swept his arm toward the door. "Now, tour?"

Blaine slid off the desk and nodded, putting his hands in his pockets. Grey noticed again that Blaine dressed very well, like an adult, but with a touch of something wild that kept it young, made it artsy. He wondered if Blaine picked his clothes himself, or if Mark chose them for him.

"Well, this is my office, as you've seen—" Grey began. Blaine followed along at his side, murmuring and asking intelligent questions about the architecture, the past campaigns displayed on the walls, joking about the drain in the bathroom floor, saying that it really could be handy and Grey should have one installed in his office, too.

Grey introduced him to his staff, the individuals who'd worked most closely with Grey on the Chill Blaine Enterprises campaign, and showed him the view from the rooftop, though he didn't linger there for long. Sure, he wanted to seduce Blaine, wanted to fuck him up against the wall right that very moment, but he knew that it had to be done right. He didn't want it to be a fast fuck, but something different, something like they should have been moving toward before his own fear and L.A. stole Blaine away from him.

Still, now in the front lobby, the simple sensation of Blaine's hand on his arm, holding him in place, took his breath away, and he had a hard time hearing Blaine's words.

"I've missed you, Grey."

Grey choked on his response. He didn't know for certain what he'd said. He thought it might've been, "Me, too."

"Do you want to go to dinner?"

"Not tonight." Grey tried to sound like it didn't hurt to turn Blaine down. "I need to finish up the boards for the presentation."

"Thursday?"

Grey licked his lips, his heart pounding out warnings, but he didn't listen. Dinner Thursday would be foolish since the pitch would be the following morning, but he found that he'd said, "Yes, Thursday."

"I'll pick you up here," Blaine said firmly.

Grey nodded. Blaine's hands slid up his arms, and he met Blaine's gaze just as Blaine's lips closed on his in a gentle kiss. Blaine's mouth was warm, tasted like cinnamon gum, and Grey sighed as Blaine's tongue touched his all too briefly.

"Grey…" Blaine nuzzled his face, and Grey's cock thickened. "I've really missed you."

"Blaine—"

"Thursday. I'll pick you up at seven."

"What about Mark?"

Blaine smiled. "Don't talk about Mark, okay? As for you and me? We're just old friends catching up, right? Nothing's happened. Until it does, I'll tell him what I need to tell him. I'm always honest with him, though. Don't complicate things, Grey. It's too soon for that."

Grey felt like a child for the first time in a long time—a chastised child who could do nothing but nod with wide eyes at the man in front of him. His hands felt cold when Blaine released them, leaving the building through the glass front doors.

Grey turned to see Amelia looking at him nervously, before she ducked her head and went back to her work. He glanced around to see several other employees watching with odd expressions. He turned on his heel and returned to his office.

CHAPTER SIX

GREY WORE A more casual outfit than usual to the office in preparation for their date. Was it a date? He wasn't sure. He only knew that he wanted it to be a date by the time the evening was over—and so it would be. The absurdity of Grey Blackburn wanting a potential hook-up with an ex to actually be a date wasn't lost on him, but as he'd been saying in various forms ever since he saw Blaine again for the first time, "Ten years is a long time. A lot can change in ten years."

Amelia smiled and told him that he looked wonderful. "So relaxed, Mr. Blackburn!"

He grinned and said, "Don't I always look wonderful, Amelia?"

"Of course," she replied, indicating the calendar on her desk. "I see that Mr. Kellerman of Chill Blaine Enterprises will be here this evening. Is there anything I need to do in preparation for the appointment?"

Grey shook his head, thumbing through some written messages she'd handed him when he first walked in. "When did the representative from Tiffany's call?"

"Seven-thirty last evening. I was still here to catch the call. I think he was surprised that I answered. He said he'd planned on leaving a message."

"Burning the midnight oil again? Be careful, Amelia—all work and no play will get you a raise, but it won't get you laid."

Amelia shrugged, blushing a little.

Grey recognized the expression and grinned predatorily. "Who was she, hmm?" he taunted.

"Nobody you'd know. A librarian—" Amelia bloomed into a happy smile. "A beautiful, wonderful, brilliant librarian, with long, brown hair and an amazing—"

"Great," Grey interrupted, dismissing any more discussion of the topic with a flip of his hand. "Happy to hear it. Just keep up the good work around here and maybe you'll get a raise to buy her a nice shiny, lezzy wedding ring or something."

Amelia rolled her eyes and shoved a folder his way. "The drafts for Chill Blaine Enterprises are in there—all they need is your approval and they'll go to the final boards."

Grey sat at his desk and tried to concentrate. Everything looked great as far as he could tell, but he was too distracted to feel confident that everything was perfect. That was what he hired the minions for, right? And it wasn't as if he hadn't held their hands every step of the way—

He picked up the nearest pen and signed off on the designs. They were as good as they were going to get.

Time dragged as he waited impatiently for the little hand to get to the seven. When the other employees left, drifting away over the course of a few hours, leaving just him and Amelia to toil, the office seemed too quiet, so he put on light music as a distraction.

The first piece was John Coltrane, and he leaned back in his seat thinking about a time in his life when he'd relaxed to techno music while eating Chinese food on the floor of his renovated loft in Nashville.

He closed his eyes, recognizing the tune of "My Favorite Things", and remembered—

—blue sheets and soft pillows, pale skin on dark fabric, red lips open with desire and crooning with need—

He shook himself like a dog, and sat up again, pulling the closest folder toward him and considered the photo of a rather ordinary looking jockstrap. He was supposed to find a way to make it pop.

—toes curling from the intensity of pleasure, eyes half-open, glazed and staring into his own—

He shifted and adjusted his cock. Jockstraps were inherently unattractive things, only made sexy by the man who filled them.

—the gentle give of a smooth shoulder under his fingers as he massaged a cramp away, soft lips on his neck, the scent of peanut butter and bananas filling the loft along with the sound of squeaking tennis shoes on the wooden floor—

Grey cradled his head in his hands and took a deep, cleansing breath, like his private yoga instructor had told him to do—right before Grey took hold of him and fucked him silly against a pile of yoga mats.

"Christ," he whispered. The longing that filled him took his breath away, making it hard to breathe. It seemed insane that he could want Blaine this much after so many years, but there it was filling him up like the tide, just a huge moving body of want, need, and *please.* "Feeling all right?"

Grey's head snapped up, and if Blaine didn't stop taking him by surprise, he wasn't going to survive the next one.

"Just thinking," he said, standing up quickly. "Wondering if you were going to be on time, or run late like you used to do. You know how I fucking hate to be kept waiting when I'm hungry." He was absolutely not hungry.

"I no longer suffer from chronic lateness syndrome," Blaine said, laughing. "Mark sees to that."

Grey moved around his desk to gather his coat. He was glad to see that Blaine wore blue jeans and a sweater under a casual jacket, meaning that they wouldn't be going anywhere fancy or boring. "And he can get you to pull away from your work, or whatever the fuck you're distracted by? I applaud the bastard. I never succeeded in that."

Blaine grinned. "He lies to me about the time. But he's even smarter—" He shoved his hands in his pockets, his eyes wandering over Grey in appraisal. "He never lies by the same amount of time, and sometimes he doesn't lie at all, so I never know if he's telling the truth or not. He keeps me on my toes."

Grey lifted his brows as he tucked his scarf in the neck of his coat. Why Blaine was telling him such things, he didn't know—and that sick tightening of his gut was definitely jealousy. Grey patted his coat, making a show of ensuring that he had his keys, before saying, "Let's go."

Blaine took the lead as they exited the Blackburn Advertising offices. Hailing a cab, he pulled Grey in after him. Conversation turned to the traditionally polite type. "How was your day?"

"Fine."

"That's good."

But Grey felt Blaine's warmth across the seat from him, and his heart beat rapidly with the proximity of him. When they pulled up to The Plaza Hotel, Grey frowned. "Not exactly the venue I was expecting," he commented as Blaine paid the fare and hopped out.

"We're staying here—Mark and I. But I got another room for tonight. You don't mind do you? It's just easier this way. We'll have privacy, get to talk, you know—get caught up."

"So, Mark will be joining us, then?" Grey asked as he followed Blaine into the beautiful, spacious lobby. The disappointment that brought was difficult to swallow around.

Blaine looked over his shoulder with an expression as though Grey had gone insane. "Of course not. I have several private rooms reserved. We'll be alone."

Grey didn't know whether or not he was relieved, so he didn't say much more as they took the elevator to the fourteenth floor. Blaine chattered politely about the weather, the hotel, the best place in town to get cupcakes, his preference for a little shop in The Village, but said nothing that required more than guttural acknowledgements from Grey.

The room itself was quite tasteful, as Grey remembered from his prior stays in the hotel, but he wasn't expecting the lowered lights, the dinner laid out nicely on a table, candles, and elegant music in the background. It was enough to break the ice, though, forcing him to laugh out loud.

"What the fuck is this? Seduction Scenes 101, or something? Christ, Blaine!"

Blaine started laughing, too, flipping on lights around the room, and turning the shitty music off. "Sorry, I told my assistants that I was bringing a special friend to the room tonight, and I suppose they just decided to prepare it in the usual way." He turned to Grey, blond hair glowing in the increased light in the room. "I get a hell of a lot of hot ass with this set up."

Grey began to unwind his scarf, still chuckling. "This attempt at romance reminds me of a time when this kid I used to fuck tried to convince me to have a picnic in Centennial park—"

Blaine grinned. "Yeah, and you know, over the years, you ended up having a lot of picnics in Centennial park with me."

Grey's heart grew warm and he smiled softly. "Yeah, I did, didn't I? Some little fucker thought it was super romantic or some shit like that."

Blaine moved toward the bed, pulled off the pillows and tossed them on the floor. "Yeah, stupid little fucker."

"Your seduction techniques have truly suffered over the years," Grey said, as Blaine ripped the coverlet off the bed, and threw it to the floor, too. "Am I supposed to begin disrobing now? Was this supposed to sweep me off my feet? Just the sight of bed sheets is supposed to give me a hard-on?"

Blaine rolled his eyes, chuckling, and Grey crossed his arms over his chest, watching as Blaine made a nest of pillows on the floor, and then as he turned to the table and began moving plates to the center of the heap.

"Well, are you going to just stand there?" Blaine asked. "Or are you going to help this old little fucker get the romantic picnic of his fucking dreams?"

Grey smirked, turned the lights back down, and joined Blaine in transferring their dinner from the table to the hotel room floor.

CHAPTER SEVEN

TWO BOTTLES OF wine later, Grey was feeling no pain, and time had seemed to rewind. He was having a picnic with his lover, both of them ten years younger, laughing like they'd never been apart.

But then the light from the candles would shift and he'd remember that despite their laughter, despite the way his body was responding to Blaine's nearness, time had indeed gone by. It'd stamped a spray of crow's feet at the corners of Blaine's eyes, and added a strength of character that only age could bring to Blaine's face.

"How's Reed?" Blaine asked, finally.

Grey had been waiting for the question for some time. He knew that it'd be the one that would lead to the intimate questions, the ones that would devolve into touching, then kissing, then fucking. It'd be the question that said, "Where is your heart in this? Here's a taste of mine."

"He's almost fourteen. I think he's gay, but I'm not sure. I've seen him looking at boys and girls, so maybe he likes both like his mom. I don't know. But he's smart, loving, kind to his mothers and excited for the sister that's coming." Grey smiled thinking of his nephew. "And he fucking knows his designers. The kid's got great taste in clothes." He laughed, before saying quietly, "I couldn't ask for more."

"I missed seeing him grow up. That makes me sad. I think of

him a lot," Blaine said. "I think of how devoted you were to him when we first met, you know? He was such a cute little baby. And then I get bummed that I missed out on a lot of his life after I left. I wish I'd kept in better touch with Fawn."

"I hear you keep in touch with Mama, though."

Blaine blushed. "She was good to me. I just call her on the important dates, though. Her birthday. Christmas. Thanksgiving."

"Last week to tell her you were in New York."

"Maybe I was fishing for information about you."

Grey's heart squeezed. "Yeah?"

"Yeah. But she never tells me much about Reed. I don't even know what he looks like now."

Grey turned and fumbled in his jacket, retrieving his phone. "I can't believe I'm doing this," he said, waking it from sleep and flipping through his photos until he found a recent one that Fawn had texted him. "Tell anyone that I have fucking pictures of my nephew in my phone, and I'll cut your balls off."

Blaine took the phone and grew very somber as he studied the photo of Reed. He looked up finally after several long minutes and Grey was surprised to see that his eyes appeared damp.

"He's beautiful. Wow. I knew he would be, but he's—" Blaine stared at the photo again before pressing the phone back into Grey's hand. "He's amazing. He looks just like you."

"That's what Fawn says, too."

"Now I'm even sorrier that I didn't see him grow up."

Grey tucked the phone back into his jacket in the ensuing silence. Part of him wanted to say, "Then why didn't you stay?"

But he knew the answer to that. Grey had been determined to lead the ultimate queer life: answering to no one, fucking tons of guys, rejection of monogamy, rejection of everything his father had stood for, including religion and love and family. Rejection of what he himself truly wanted deep down, even. He'd been such an angry young man.

Besides, even if Blaine had wanted to stay, had really wanted to give their relationship another good old college try, Grey would never have allowed it. He'd made sure that when Blaine left, it was under circumstances that he'd stay away for good. It'd nearly killed him to do it. The things he'd said, the things he'd done…

He'd always claimed that saying sorry was bullshit, but as he'd aged he'd begun to recognize the value of confession and absolution. The day that he'd accepted Reed's tearful, tweenage apology for calling him a fucking faggot, it'd occurred to him that forgiveness didn't make a person into a victim. Asking for absolution wasn't about shirking consequences. Sometimes asking for forgiveness and granting it was the ultimate act of taking responsibility.

Not everyone was like his father.

"Blaine, I said some things, a long time ago…" He really wanted to make it right, find a way to let Blaine know that this time would be different. "I didn't—"

"Shhh," Blaine whispered. "Don't go there."

They sat, not speaking, and Grey took another sip from his almost empty glass.

"Grey?"

He met Blaine's eyes and held the gaze.

"Grey, can I—?"

"Yes."

Blaine's mouth was hungry, devouring his with sharp nips and bites. Grey leaned back to the floor, pulling Blaine with him as he went.

CHAPTER EIGHT

B LAINE'S CALVES RUBBED against Grey's sides as they rutted together. Shirts, pants, and underwear had been hastily discarded in a heap beside them. The blankets they were sitting on didn't provide much cushion, but Grey couldn't take his hands or his mouth off Blaine long enough to try to gentle their movements with pillows or to shift their activity to the bed.

Grey was frantic to get inside of Blaine, as though if he could just press his cock into Blaine's tight body, he could make everything right, erase everything that had gone so wrong. He knew nothing could reverse time, but the heat between them, the lust that made him feel insane, could block out the past and make it irrelevant.

His hand found Blaine's asshole, and his mouth covered Blaine's lips to capture the moan when he pressed two fingers inside. It was tight, hot, and silky smooth. His cock jerked with desire, and he twisted his fingers, trying to open Blaine, unlock him physically and emotionally. He wanted to look up and see the familiar softness in Blaine's eyes, the look of love and affection that he'd missed so deeply. Yet he feared that it wouldn't be there, so he kept his eyes focused on his fingers.

"Hold on," Blaine grunted, grabbing Grey's hands and stilling his motions. "Lube. Condoms."

Blaine broke free, pushing Grey's still grasping hands away, moving on his hands and knees toward a black bag placed strategically by the bedside. Grey, impatient and so hard that his cock leaked pre-cum down into his pubic hair, didn't wait for Blaine to return, instead approaching him from behind and pushing him to the floor by the side of the bed, the rough carpet leaving red marks on Blaine's pale skin.

Grey spread Blaine's ass cheeks and buried his face in Blaine's sweet, hot crack, licking his hole, nipping and shoving his tongue into him, loving the taste, which was absolutely the same, and completely familiar to him. He couldn't get enough. He held Blaine's hips, pulling his ass firmly to his lips, and rimmed him hard and fast, giving him everything he could. Blaine writhed and bucked against the carpet, his rough voice crying out in pleasure.

Grey didn't stop until he heard Blaine's breath catching in near sobs and then, holding Blaine's hips steady, Grey pulled back. He reached into the black bag and found the lube and condom. He made quick work of sliding the condom on and squirting lube on Blaine's asshole.

"Fuck me," Blaine muttered. "Fuck me, please."

Grey couldn't wait any longer. He drove into Blaine, both of them arching and crying out as his cock cleaved Blaine open. He was too tight and Grey had to stop for a moment, bend his head to Blaine's back and catch his breath. Blaine moaned beneath him, obviously struggling to accommodate his girth and Grey tried to hold back, but finally the need to move overrode his ability to resist, and he thrust into Blaine again and again.

The friction of thrusting his cock into Blaine's tight ass was nearly too intense for pleasure. But when Blaine pushed back groaning, asking for more, Grey couldn't have stopped if he wanted to. He nuzzled the back of Blaine's neck and took deep breaths of his scent, familiar, though strange from different soap and cologne. He slid his hands up Blaine's body and wrapped them around Blaine's shoulders, panting as they strained together.

"Fuck," Blaine gasped. "Oh fuck."

Grey pulled back, angled his thrust and bit his lower lip as Blaine shouted and jerked beneath him. Glancing over his shoulder, Grey saw Blaine's toes curling and uncurling spasmodically as Grey fucked him harder and harder. Blaine's hands gripped at the carpet but couldn't get a good hold of the short threads. His knuckles were skinned and red from the effort.

When Blaine reached beneath himself to grasp his own cock, Grey knocked his hand away, instead pushing his hips into the carpet and forcing Blaine to rut against the roughness. "Grey, oh God, so fucking *good*," Blaine whimpered, his face also rubbing against the rug with each push of Grey's cock into him.

Blaine's body wasn't as lithe, he wasn't as young, but he still fit Grey perfectly, arching under him in exact rhythm, no effort in their joining beyond the strain to reach orgasm, or to postpone it for as long as possible.

Grey buried his nose in the top of Blaine's sweat-damp hair, and slid his hands from Blaine's shoulders down to his hands, gripped them, and then pulled his arms closed, wrapping them both together as he continued to fuck with strong, almost vicious thrusts. Blaine writhed under him, trying to get purchase with his knees to thrust his ass up.

"Grey," Blaine begged, his voice raw sounding. "Fuck, I need to come."

Grey couldn't stop thrusting as he held Blaine tightly. It built hard and fast. His balls tightened, and he jerked as he slammed into Blaine. "Fuck," he whispered into Blaine's hair as he came.

He shuddered, panting hard, and trying to see through the blue and black spots swirling in front of his eyes. He felt Blaine's ass squeezing his dick and realized that the shuddering, low moans were from Blaine's orgasm, and held on as Blaine shook beneath him.

Finally able to breath, his body utterly wrung out and sore, he rolled them onto their sides and pulled free. His cock was spent, and his condom full. He carefully tied it off, throwing it toward a trashcan he could vaguely make out by the desk across the room. Blaine was still breathing hard, and Grey wrapped his arms around him, soothing him with soft strokes up and down his stomach and chest.

"God, Grey." Blaine turned in Grey's arms and his eyes were glassy, stunned, and very blue. "In-fucking-credible. I'd almost forgotten. Christ."

Grey hummed and cleared his throat, trying to find words. "Fucking hot. That was—" he broke off and changed his mind. "*You're* fucking hot."

It had felt amazing to be inside of Blaine again. He wished he were still hard so that he could slide back into Blaine's heat and stay there. His lips brushed over Blaine's neck and shoulders, and he closed his eyes, just feeling Blaine's skin under his fingertips.

Blaine moved against him and when Grey looked up, he saw the soft eyes that he'd wanted to see, needed to see. For the last ten years he'd dreamed of seeing that expression again. "Blaine—"

"I've missed you so much, Grey. Fuck. So much."

Grey nodded, slung his leg over Blaine's hips and maneuvered them both until his lips hovered over Blaine's. He breathed the words, "Missed you, too," and took Blaine's lips gently, kissing him until he felt heat rising between them again. He pulled away, glancing down at Blaine's cock. It was still half-hard, and rug burns from the carpet graced Blaine's hipbones and thighs. Looking again at Blaine's face, he saw that a red mark was rubbed into his cheek as well.

His lips moved across Blaine's skin, kissing the marks that he could find, sucking a few more into Blaine's inner thighs where his scent was strong and the taste of his come could be detected.

Soon Blaine was hard and almost begging again, his eyes glazed and his mouth bright red, hanging open and needy. Grey found the lube quickly and slicked three fingers, working them into Blaine's asshole. Then he licked Blaine's perineum and up to his balls, mouthing them as Blaine cursed, grasping Grey's hair and begging him to suck his straining cock.

Grey took the head of Blaine's cock into his mouth, tonguing the crown and the slit, and used his free hand to hold Blaine's hip steady. Overriding his lover's natural urge to slam his dick down Grey's throat, he took his time. He twisted his fingers in Blaine's ass, found his prostate and tapped it in the same rhythm as he sucked Blaine's cock. He dove down, letting it hit the back of his throat. Saliva spilled from his mouth, running down and over Blaine's balls and into his ass crack, helping to lube Grey's fingers as they fucked his hole.

"Grey, Grey, oh God, *Grey*, oh God, *fuck*," Blaine chanted, his hips struggling to surge up, but Grey held him firmly, sucking as hard as he could, feeling the tight skin of Blaine's cock throb against his lips and tongue. "Shit, oh fuck, oh *shit*, oh!" Blaine froze, and Grey sucked harder. The pulse of Blaine's orgasm rose under his velvety shaft, and Blaine cried out harshly, his ass gripping Grey's fingers, and his hands convulsing in Grey's hair.

Grey drained Blaine's cock, and then pulled away, ran his hands soothingly up and down Blaine's body, before reaching for a condom. Blaine's blue eyes were huge and sex-dazed as Grey lifted his calves up to his shoulders, and positioned his cock at Blaine's hole.

Staring into Blaine's eyes, Grey pushed in slowly, taking his time, working his way in. He studied Blaine's expressions, marking the hiss of pain at the stretch, the slutty blink, and sexy lip-lick of desire. And then he heard the murmured words that he'd missed for much too long, "I love you. I do."

Grey couldn't look away as he gently, firmly, honestly made love to Blaine again for the first time in ten years.

• • •

HOURS LATER THEY lay in the bed on sweat-damp sheets. Blaine sprawled on his back, exhausted, and Grey watched Blaine through half-closed eyes. His brain was too buzzed on endorphins to think clearly, but something nagged at him. Something that sounded like, "Don't fool yourself. It can't be this simple."

He'd learned a long time ago that nothing can be cured, fixed, or even proclaimed with sex. Even if his body spoke more clearly than any words he could find, that wasn't good enough.

Still, he couldn't escape the lazy, drugged feeling of having just fucked Blaine silly three times—or was it four? And if he counted the time that he hadn't been able to come, but Blaine had, then he supposed that it might even have been five.

Blaine sighed and ran his hands over his face, sitting up and looking around the room with an expression of confusion. "God, what time is it?"

Grey glanced at the clock by the bed. "Two-thirty."

"Crap."

Suddenly Grey's sense of warm and lazy was replaced with a chill that reached his bones.

"Somewhere you have to be?" Grey asked, as nonchalantly as possible, but obviously failing because Blaine turned to him with a slightly wounded expression.

"Yes. I—" Blaine ran his hand through his hair and over his face. "I don't want to go. But, I need to. Well, in about fifteen minutes, so that I can get cleaned up before I go back to Mark. We have a very open relationship but part of that agreement is a curfew when we're in the same city. He'll expect me by three."

Grey nodded and began to roll out of bed.

"Grey, wait. Please. This wasn't just a fuck to you, was it?" Blaine pulled his knees up to his chest, and Grey thought he looked just like the twenty year old he'd taken home so long ago. "Because it wasn't to me."

Grey measured his words for a moment. He knew if he answered truthfully then he was going to open himself up to being devastatingly hurt. But if he lied, then he'd never have a chance to be with Blaine in the way he wanted. "You know it wasn't. Just a fuck, I mean. It was so much more than that to me."

Blaine nodded, his eyes down and his expression sad.

Grey relaxed back into the bed and finally said, "You love him. I know that you love him."

"Yeah," he replied quietly. "I do. But not the way—he's not—" Blaine met Grey's gaze. "He's not the love of my life. He knows he isn't. I've never lied to him about that and I even tried to end it with him several times because I know I mean more to him than he does to me. But he's stubborn and said he'd take me as long as he could have me."

"I get that."

"Yeah. He's like, I don't know, my best friend, my business partner with benefits, or something. It's warm but not passionate. I don't feel for him the way I feel for—felt for you."

Grey swallowed hard and voiced his fear. "Nothing feels like first love, but that doesn't mean your first love is right for you in the end."

Blaine didn't seem satisfied with that comment, asking, "Have you ever loved anyone the way that you loved me? Can you look at me and say that what we had wasn't the right thing at the wrong time?"

"No," Grey answered, his tongue thick but somehow managing the words. "It was right. But you were young and I was afraid to commit, scared of what it meant to love you. I was an idiot. A mean, stupid idiot."

"Yeah, well, that's a given." Blaine relaxed a little, almost smiling, but then he tensed again almost immediately. "You hurt me. I knew how much you loved me and yet you wouldn't even consider coming to L.A. with me. You acted like I wasn't worth following. Like fighting for me, for us, wasn't an option. You just said good luck, kissed me, cussed me out, and then let me go on my merry fucking way like it wasn't cruel to do that to me."

Grey couldn't look at him. He knew what he'd done, what he'd said, and he knew why he'd done it. But the man who'd always said that he'd never be in Blaine's way, never be someone who kept Blaine from becoming the best, most successful man he could be, definitely regretted his choice to sacrifice his own happiness for what he'd thought was Blaine's. As he'd aged he'd seen that it hadn't been necessary, that Blaine could have still had L.A., and success, and Grey, too.

But it hadn't seemed like that at the time. Not to his bitter, angry, fear-clouded mind, at least.

"I guess what I'm still pissed about is that now, if I leave Mark, I'm going to be doing the same thing to him that you did to me. And it didn't have to be that way. We could have been together all this time." Blaine's lips trembled.

"Why didn't you—" Grey started, but quit at Blaine's incredulous look.

"Fight for you?" Blaine asked. "I fought for you from the time I was twenty until I was twenty-four. But you were like a puzzle box I couldn't ever get open. Was I supposed to beg you to want me enough that you'd follow me? Was I wrong to want you to be the one to fight for me for a change?"

"No."

"It hurt like hell for me to see that coldness in your eyes, like I was just someone passing through."

"Like you said, you were twenty-four. I didn't want to hold you back."

"So you said at the time. The truth was you were too scared to risk it with me. You chose being alone over putting your whole life on the line for an adventure with me."

"It was a lot to ask," Grey muttered. "Moving to L.A. with you, starting over? I had just started really making headway with my firm—"

"It was the perfect time to branch out."

"It wasn't." Grey's throat tightened, the truth burning there. "But I should have done it all the same."

Blaine's mouth worked. When he spoke, it sounded like he could barely breathe to say the words. "It took me a long time to forgive you. A really fucking long time, and by then I was with Mark. Being with him helped me realize that what happened at the end with us? It wasn't about me at all. It was about you. I thought you didn't think I was worth it, but now I know the truth. You didn't think *you* were worth it. You were just too scared to take the leap with me."

"Terrified. But I leapt eventually." Grey smiled grimly. "Not to L.A. but I'm here in New York. And right now I've leapt into bed with you."

Blaine's mouth twitched sadly. "True. Probably I shouldn't

let you back into my life." He scratched at his head, frowning. "But I know I'll always want you. Across continents and time, I'll want you."

Grey's heart raced. "Yeah?"

"So maybe it's time to give up some of my fucking pride and ask if you're willing to do the same." Blaine ran his hands over his face and scooted to the edge of the bed. "Damn. I know this sucks, but I can't talk about this now. I have to go. No matter what happens next, I owe him this much—keeping to our agreement."

He moved away from the bed, stepping gingerly, and Grey knew that Blaine could still feel the fucks they'd just shared.

Blaine said quietly, "You can stay here tonight if you want. Or you can call a car. I'll have my assistants pay your way."

Grey watched Blaine dress. A series of shields descended over Blaine's face with each item of clothing, and Grey wondered if he'd dreamed their whole conversation. Maybe he was another random fuck to Blaine after all.

Until Blaine turned to him, hand on the doorknob, and said, "I want to be with you, Grey. Now and in the future. But I have to go for now. In the meantime, you need to decide what you want, because if we do this thing? This time it's for good, Grey. Forever."

Then he was gone back to his lover as Grey fought off waves of elation and panic, before calling for a car back home.

CHAPTER NINE

MARK VANDERHALDER SAT across from Grey appearing relaxed and excited. His handsome face nearly glowed. "Blaine is looking forward to seeing your work, Mr. Blackburn. I'm sorry he couldn't be here this morning. He had a very late night and I insisted that he sleep in. But, please, begin your pitch. I've been given authority to make the final decision on this campaign, so you've only got to impress *me*, and I'm easy." Mark smiled and leaned forward, his hands clasped on the table. "And please feel free to make the obvious joke."

Grey smirked and opened the files in front of him. He wasn't sure what to think of Blaine's absence from the meeting. He told himself that Blaine didn't want to deal with seeing him and Mark in the same room together so soon, and with so much up in the air. But part of him was convinced that Blaine had rethought the whole thing, had returned to his hotel room, found his lover sleeping, and reconsidered his promise to Grey.

He blocked those thoughts from his mind and went on auto-pilot, gliding through the presentation with his typical wit and hardline truths. Mark's eyes grew wider and brighter as Grey talked, nodding enthusiastically.

"Mr. Blackburn, this is *exactly* what Chill Blaine Enterprises has needed for a long time. When Dominique began singing your praises, I admit I was skeptical at first. But once I saw what you'd done for her company, I just knew that you were the right man for us. And, well, can I say that I'm happy to have been proven right?"

Grey lifted his shoulders in mock embarrassment. "Please, Mr. Vanderhalder, you'll make me blush."

Everyone laughed and all that was left was to arrange an appointment for contracts to be executed.

"Sometime next week will have to do," Mark commented. "I have to make a run to L.A. for a few days to oversee a project." He leaned forward conspiratorially. "And grab some of Blaine's winter clothes. He never packs properly on his own and fall is coming to New York early this year."

"Indeed," Grey agreed, smiling with what he hoped was a measure of sincerity he didn't feel.

Images of Mark packing clothes from a closet filled with his and Blaine's things filled Grey's mind and ate at his stomach. If he were a different man, he'd have thought the sensation was guilt.

Mark's cell phone rang and he gestured with his hand to indicate that he'd only be a moment before he walked to the corner of the room to take the call. Grey's assistant, Amelia, worked with Mark's assistant, Rose, to schedule a time to meet the following week while Grey eavesdropped on Mark's conversation.

"It's okay, baby. I've got it all under control. The pitch? Oh, you'll love it. It's perfect. No, it's amazing."

Baby? Grey rolled his eyes.

"Sure. Well, you know I'll be in L.A., but you could still—" Mark nodded, using one finger to plug his other ear, like he was having a hard time hearing Blaine. "Okay, sure. I'll let Mr. Blackburn know. Absolutely. No, you won't regret it, baby. Best fucking pitch I've ever seen."

Out of the corner of his eye, Grey saw Mark's gaze shift to him, and so he strove to look busy shifting his papers around on the conference table. He had to strain to hear the next bit and wished that he could tell Amelia and Mark's assistant to shut the fuck up.

"He's hot, too. Maybe I'll fuck him. Think he's into quickies with clients?" Mark didn't sound like he was kidding, and a strange bubble of panic started in Grey's stomach. He didn't know what to do, didn't know what Blaine expected of him. The old Grey Blackburn, the one Blaine had fallen in love with, would have fucked this Mark guy without question.

But it'd been ten years, and a lot could change in ten years. The idea of fucking Blaine's lover, the man who was going to go to their home and pack clothes for Blaine to wear in wintry New York, didn't sit right with him.

The end of the conversation was blocked by Amelia laughing at something Mark's assistant said, and Grey seriously considered firing her.

When Mark returned to the table, he was smiling but there was, thankfully, no flirtation. Grey was relieved but wondered what Blaine had said to throw Mark off the hunt. Had he told the truth?

There was no hint of that on Mark's face either, though, and Grant was surprised to find he was disappointed.

●　●　●

"I TOLD YOU, Grey. This was a huge mistake. What the fuck were you thinking?" The sound of Jamie's foster sons yelling in the background was very distracting. Not that Grey minded given the way the conversation was going.

"Jamie, you've lied to me all these years."

"What? What are you talking about?"

"You always said you're my baby brother, but you're really a Jewish mother, aren't you? Admit it." Grey shoved back in his desk chair and propped his feet on his desk.

"I'm just being cautious. Remember the way Fawn and I had to pick up the pieces last time?" Grey could just imagine Jamie standing with his arms crossed over his chest, frown fixed firmly in place.

Grey jerked the phone away from his ear as Jamie yelled, "Dammit, Matthew! Don't kick your brother!"

Grey rolled his eyes. "Listen, we'll discuss it when you don't have a house full of pants shitters."

"That's Jarrod. Matthew never shits his pants."

"Good to know that a seven year old can use the bathroom responsibly."

"He's six."

"Whatever. I have to go. Later."

Grey disconnected the phone, gathered his things, and prepared to leave. He hadn't heard from Blaine since the night they'd fucked, and it had been nearly two days. Not that he'd texted or called Blaine, either. But since Blaine was the one in a relationship, open or not, the ball was naturally in his court. Grey knew that Mark had left town, though, and the agony of waiting for Blaine to text or call ramped up by the minute. Maybe he'd been just another fuck after all.

He stepped out into the chilly autumn night and headed toward the subway. The train was delayed due to some technical difficulty and he listened to a guy playing a flute on the opposite platform while he waited. The heavy scent of human flesh pressed underground without sufficient ventilation filled his lungs.

If he were back in Nashville, he'd head over to the diner, and Mama would serve him some coffee and some unsolicited advice. He missed his mother. They didn't always get along, but he could count on her to give him hard to hear truths. And a slap or two of affection.

Their relationship difficulties were as much his fault as hers. He'd pushed her away when he needed her most, and his father's beatings had left her as terrorized as he'd been. Eventually, she'd gotten free, though, and she'd tried to stand up for him. A little too late, but she'd tried.

Still, she was his mother, and he loved her.

He loved that even though, he, Jamie and Caldwell could afford to let her retire in style, she insisted on keeping her job at the diner. It gave her life, she claimed. Kept her in touch with people and their humanity. Mama was a fighter.

He almost pulled out his cell phone to call her, but knew that once he had her on the line he wouldn't have the words to explain. He'd just make her worry if he did that. Grey didn't like to make Mama worry because then she nagged him about everything—about coming to visit, about seeing Reed more often, about being a better man.

Mama could be a big pain in the ass. Maybe he didn't miss her as much as he thought.

When the train arrived, Grey didn't sit, preferring to stand. Staring into space, he remembered soft, pale skin and deep, throaty groans. He lost time and finally became aware that he'd missed his stop for the first time in the two years he'd lived in New York. He got off at the next opportunity. He climbed the stairs toward fresh night air, and several blocks later he found himself standing at Fifth and Central Park South, staring up at the bright lights of The Plaza Hotel.

Grey approached the desk in the lobby with his chin up, fully prepared to fuck the guy behind the counter if that's what it took to get Blaine's room number. "Grey Blackburn to see Mr. Blaine Kellerman," he said imperiously, having noted from a young age that an attitude of entitlement often makes seduction unnecessary.

"Of course, sir," the young man said, picking up the phone and pressing in a few numbers. "There's a Mr. Grey Blackburn here for Mr. Kellerman, sir," he spoke into the receiver, met Grey's eyes and smiled. Apparently there would be no need to fuck the guy to get the information he needed. "Right away. Thank you."

Grey smiled in return, intending to appear gracious but not caring if it came across as impatient. The young man ran a key card through a magnetizer and Grey took it from his outstretched hand.

"Mr. Kellerman is expecting you." He showed him the room number on the card. "Have a good evening, sir."

Grey nodded, his heart trip-hammering in his chest. Now that he was here, he realized he had no idea what to say, or if Blaine even wanted to see him. It'd been instinct, an irresistible impulse that'd brought him here. An impulse born of the dreadful hope seeing Blaine and making love to him had reawakened.

The elevator carried him inexorably closer to his goal and his hands began sweating. He had the ludicrous thought that he should have brought flowers to help him plead his case. He shook his head at the complete and utter lesbian he'd apparently become in the ten years he'd been away from Blaine. Still, roses might not have been a bad idea, and he could still turn around, go down the block and buy some. It was a perfectly reasonable thing to do, really. And, maybe he wouldn't buy them after all. Maybe he'd just keep walking, get back on the subway, and—

The elevator doors slid open and he stepped into the hallway, wiped his hands on his pants, and found the room. He stared at the number and raised his hand to knock. It wasn't too late to get the roses or go home.

Who was he kidding? Grey snorted. It was far too late.

CHAPTER TEN

B LAINE HELD THE door open, his blue button-up shirt open to the waist, a provocative line of pale skin drawing Grey's eyes.

"I didn't think you were going to come," Blaine said, leaning against the doorjamb. "I'd nearly given up."

"The elevator did seem to take a fucking long time," Grey murmured.

Blaine chuckled. "I meant—" He looked into Grey's eyes and shook his head. "Never mind."

Grey followed him into the room, his mouth dry and his cock already half-hard. Blaine's hand gesture of topic dismissal suddenly clued him in to the fact that this had been a test of sorts. That Blaine had been waiting for days for him to come. What was it that Blaine had wanted from him and that he'd always refused to give? He'd wanted Grey to fight for him.

Grey sighed. "I wish I could say that I was being deliberately obtuse, but I've never been good at fucking relationship games."

"Don't insult yourself, Grey. You've always been good at fucking and at games. It's the relationship part that you struggle with."

Grey threw off his coat and sat down opposite Blaine on the sofa. "I was giving you space. I thought, with Mark, the ball should be in your court."

"Convenient for you, isn't it? You don't even have to try."

"That's not what I meant and you know it. Don't twist things around on me."

Blaine shrugged and picked up the remote control, saying coolly, "I was getting ready to watch some television. Do you want to join me?"

Grey blinked in confusion. He tried to figure out what sort of test *this* might be. His head ached and he rubbed at his eyes.

Blaine began to flip through the channels. Somehow even the way he pushed the button on the remote control seemed angry.

If relationship tests were the kind of bullshit Blaine had in store for him, he'd fail every time. And maybe Jamie had been right after all. Maybe Blaine *had* changed, because ten years was a long time and—

"Fine, Grey," Blaine said, putting the remote back down. "Why don't you tell me what you came here for? Did you want to fuck again? Was that what you wanted? I'm sure I can provide a nice orgasm—"

"No," Grey spoke quietly. "No. I came here because I wanted to be near you. Though considering the fucking twat attitude you're copping right now, I'm not quite sure why."

Blaine's eyebrows went up. Then he laughed. "I *am* being a twat, aren't I?"

Grey didn't bother answering.

"You're right, Grey. I'm being a twat. I wanted you to come running over here the morning after we fucked, and instead you waited two days. Long enough for me to put up what Mark calls my 'infamous defenses'. Now you're here, you came because you wanted to be with me, which was exactly what I wanted from you, and I'm treating you like crap."

Grey sighed heavily. This was kind of thing that he'd always hated about the relationships he'd observed over the years. The manipulation, the guilt-trips, and worse. Maybe deciding to try again with Blaine had been a bad idea after all.

"But, you know what?" Blaine's voice was soft now, and Grey looked over to see him smiling warmly. "I'm not really that guy. That's just who I am when I'm scared."

"I applaud your therapist," Grey said, sarcastically.

Blaine grinned. "She's great. Want her number?" Then he leaned back comfortably and said, "Okay, let's see—we could try talking for a minute. What've you been up to the last few days?"

Grey looked into Blaine's eyes and decided to be honest. "Fucking wondering what the hell I've done letting myself be with you. And then wondering when the fuck I can do it again. And freaking out that you hadn't texted or called. Wondering if you wanted me again, too."

"How about now? What are you thinking about now?"

"Blaine, I guess it's time that you and I have a serious—"

"I may die a young and highly unnatural death if I'm about to hear Grey Blackburn say that we need to talk."

Grey smirked. "Where's the phone? I'll go ahead and call 911 before I say the words."

Blaine let loose with a death gargle and slid down off the couch, with his eyes rolling back and his tongue hanging out.

Grey couldn't help but laugh. He prodded Blaine's hip with his toe until Blaine sat up, sighed, and waved his hands between them. "Let's talk then."

Grey took a deep breath. He hadn't planned anything in particular, but the last two days and the sales pitch with Mark had brought hundreds of questions to the surface. "How can you leave something good with Mark for God-knows-what with me? When you know that I'm fucking terrible at this?"

Blaine nodded and appeared to be seriously considering the question. "I've wondered the same thing. Mark and I are very comfortable, and I love him. I've considered not ending things with Mark, seeing if you'd be interested in coming in as a third with us, but—" Blaine broke off.

Grey's gut twisted. He had no problem with polyamory except when it came to the idea of sharing Blaine with anyone. Then he felt like he might be sick.

Blaine went on, his breath hitching slightly. "Have you ever read anything about Valentino and Giancarlo Giametti? Once lovers, now business partners and best friends?"

"Blaine if you're getting ready to compare your relationship with Mark to Valentino and Giancarlo, then I'm going to have to go now, because you are clearly fucking delusional."

"Give me a minute, Grey," Blaine held up his hand. "The thing is, Mark and I will never be devoted at the level of Giancarlo and Valentino, but we have a relationship that isn't impossible to negotiate as non-lovers."

"You live together. He takes care of you. He's scampered across the country to bring back your winter clothes. I won't ever be that guy."

"I don't actually need that guy," Blaine replied seriously. "I can take care of myself, you know."

"But obviously you wanted that guy if—"

"No, I fell into it. Mark was there. He wanted to take care of me. I was busy, so I let him." Blaine shrugged.

Grey closed his eyes and rubbed his hands together. "I really just want to fuck you and take you home with me."

"You could do that."

"It can't be that simple."

Blaine sighed. "No. It can't be. Mark's feelings for me are..."

"He loves you."

"He does. But not like you love me."

"What does that even mean?" Grey made himself ask. "We don't even know if we can get along, Blaine. You have to know going into this that I haven't changed all that much. I'm still the shit-head I've always been."

"I hope so."

"Jesus, what the fuck are you thinking leaving this guy for me?" Grey wanted to stop his mouth, but his need to protect Blaine kept the words spilling out. "After one night? After a few fucks?"

Blaine stood calmly. The only evidence that he was discomfited was the shaking fingers that rose to tug his earlobe. "You were always going on about me taking risks, Grey. Encouraging me, pushing me to do it. Saying that I couldn't pussy out on my future no matter how scary. You pushed me to be the kind of guy who could go to L.A. and conquer."

"I'm so proud of you."

"I know. And I won't apologize for the fact that I'm willing to walk away from a relationship that is entirely less idyllic than it appears from the outside looking in." Blaine's eyes softened and he said seriously, "I don't want to regret you for the rest of my life."

"You'll regret me more being with me."

"After all this time, I'd hoped you would've found something inside yourself that you believed was worthy of love, Grey."

"Fuck the therapy bullshit, Blaine."

"I'm onto you. I always have been."

Grey moved forward, grabbing Blaine's arms and pulling him into a fierce kiss. He wanted Blaine, and he wanted him safe, he wanted him close, and he feared he'd ruin everything because he was a fucking idiot who couldn't do love right.

"Grey," Blaine said, his head turned to the side as Grey

sucked kisses into the curve of his neck. "Let's take it one step at a time. It'll be like fucking."

Grey met Blaine's eyes. "Like fucking?"

"Just like fucking."

Grey had no idea what Blaine was talking about, but he didn't care. He picked Blaine up, carried him to the bedroom of the suite, and flung him on the bed. "I can do fucking."

•　•　•

BLAINE WRITHED UNDER him, moaning and running his fingernails down Grey's arms.

Every thrust brought Grey closer to orgasm, but he held back, wanting to make sure that Blaine came first. He twined his hands in Blaine's hair and used it for leverage to deepen the strokes.

Blaine cried out and Grey lowered his mouth to Blaine's neck, lapping at the pool of sweat in the hollow of his throat. He slid his lips to Blaine's ear and whispered, "I want to fuck you forever."

Blaine's beautiful, perfect reply was to arch his back and come.

•　•　•

BLAINE CURLED IN Grey's arms, his fingers trembling with exhaustion when he tweaked Grey's nipple.

Grey ran his hand over Blaine's sweat-damp hair and whispered, "Okay?"

"Fuck yeah."

Grey smiled, sated and tired. "Sleep awhile?"

"Yeah."

He drew the sheet over them both. Grey spooned behind

Blaine and closed his eyes. An odd lump in his throat made it hard to swallow.

Christ, it was so good to be home.

CHAPTER ELEVEN

Apparently step one in the "relationships are just like fucking" handbook was for Blaine to call Mark and tell him to ship the winter clothes and to stay put in L.A. for a while.

Actually, he supposed it was step two, because step one was to fuck again—repeatedly.

"I'm with someone and I've always promised to tell you if one of my dalliances became more than a hook-up. And it has. This can't even be called a dalliance, even. It's beyond that," Blaine said, pacing by the windows while Grey listened from the bed.

"The truth is, I want to see how it goes with this man." He grimaced. "Of course, I love you, Mark. Christ, I'll always love you, but that isn't what this is about." He sighed and sat down at the little table by the window, his robe hanging open. "I've been nothing if not honest with you from the start. I love you, but there's always been the possibility that I could fall in love with someone else and want to move on."

Grey winced when Blaine said, "You're right. You deserve better than this and you always have. I agree." There was a long silence and then Blaine continued, "I'll have the concierge and front desk keep an eye out for the box. Thanks for sending those things. I'll talk to you about the new project tomorrow, okay?"

Then his voice went soft and gentle. "Don't cry, sweetheart. I promise, there's someone out there who will deserve your love. That someone isn't me."

Blaine's face was pale when he climbed into bed, and Grey didn't know what to say, so he reached out and pulled him close. "He was kind of upset," Blaine said softly.

"I gathered."

They sat in silence for a while. Blaine broke it by saying, "Because I don't love him that way, I wish he didn't love me so much."

"You're easy to love," Grey whispered, saying too much.

Blaine snorted. "I'm a bastard, actually."

"Really? I never imagined your mother as the getting-pregnant-out-of-wedlock type."

Blaine chuckled. "You shouldn't make me laugh. It's not nice. I should at least feel bad about hurting him for a few hours, don't you think?"

"Sure, if you want to. Or we could make you feel really good, and then you won't think about it at all." Grey slid his hand down Blaine's chest, over his stomach, down to his hardening cock. "I love the way you move under me."

"I'm pretty good at moving over people, too. And in them, as well. Wanna see?"

Grey smirked. "You're taking advantage of the fact that I feel sorry for you right now, aren't you?"

"Yes."

Grey stroked his hair, gazing into his eyes.

Blaine smiled softly and kissed his lips. "But only if you want to."

Grey cleared his throat. "Okay, well—take it slow. It's been a very long time."

• • •

WHEN HE SAID it had been a long time, he meant that it had been ten years. Despite the fact that even Grey Blackburn loved to be fucked sometimes, he'd never been able to open himself up in that way for anyone after he'd forced Blaine to leave. Somehow the years with Blaine made certain parts of sex seem like *more* than just a physical release.

Now on his stomach with Blaine's chin digging into his shoulder blade, he concentrated on relaxing enough for Blaine to push inside. He wished they were face-to-face, but the height differential limited the positions they could comfortably screw in.

When the burn from the stretch forced a gasp from deep inside, he buried his face in the pillow glad Blaine couldn't see his expression. He felt too vulnerable to cope and didn't want Blaine to know how scared he really was inside.

But he'd forgotten how Blaine could read his body, and the soothing sound of Blaine's voice joined the gentling strokes down his side.

"Shh, relax. Relax."

Grey sighed and spread his legs wider. His ass throbbed where Blaine filled him, and he imagined he could feel his heartbeat thudding against Blaine's dick. He breathed deeply, moaning as Blaine slid further in on each exhale.

His hole twitched and pushed against Blaine's intrusion. When Blaine pulled slowly back, and then thrust forward hard, Grey's head lifted from the pillow and he bit down on his lip, trying not to cry out. Blaine's pubic hair grazed Grey's ass, and he lowered his head back down, trembling, waiting for the final thrust to bring Blaine flush.

But it didn't come.

Instead Blaine brushed his lips over Grey's shoulders, lifted his head to reach Grey's neck, and held perfectly still. Grey's pulse rushed in his veins, filling his ears, so that he could barely hear.

Blaine whispered against his damp skin, "God, you're tight. Fuck, I can feel your pulse on my dick." Blaine bit his shoulder then licked it gently. "It's making me crazy."

Grey didn't reply. He tried to hold on to the moment, and not slip away into the sensation. He felt Blaine's cock jerk, and knew that Blaine wasn't going to last. He squeezed his eyes shut and slid his knees higher, getting leverage to force himself back, taking the last several inches of Blaine's dick inside, fast and hard. He threw his head back, and twisted his hips. Blaine grabbed his pelvis and tried to force him to stop moving.

"Don't. Don't—fuck!" Blaine gasped, his cock pulsing in Grey's ass. "Fuck!"

Grey smiled into the pillow, saying, "You never could wait to come."

Blaine's breath was heavy against his back, and Grey chuckled when sharp teeth closed on the skin right over his spine in retaliation for the comment. After a minute of rest, Blaine pulled out slowly, Grey looked over his shoulder, watching Blaine clutch the base of the condom and then dispose of it.

Then Blaine grabbed another condom with a flourish and rolled it on his still hard dick. Grey's heart beat at a reckless speed when Blaine met his eye, slapped Grey's ass, and pulled his cheeks apart. "You're going to pay for that, Grey."

Blaine's voice was controlled, but he was rough in pulling Grey's hips up. Grey grabbed the pillow to steady himself. Blaine's thrust in wasn't careful at all, and Grey's head snapped up when Blaine's balls slapped his ass.

"Now we'll see who can't wait to come," Blaine muttered, rolling his hips with firm, deep strokes.

Grey wanted to answer, to make a smart-ass comment back, but his mouth was unable to form words. Blaine's cock plowed into him without mercy. Blaine's hands held Grey steady, his fingernails digging into the grooves of Grey's hips, creating sharp flecks of pain in the midst of unbelievable, hot, straining pleasure.

Grey's fists clenched the pillow and he lifted his ass as much as he could, trying to take Blaine's thrusts more easily. He grunted when the angle forced the head of Blaine's cock over his prostate. He tried to gain some purchase with his knees to claim some control over the pace, but Blaine shifted forward, using his thighs to push Grey's legs further apart, opening him and fucking him even more deeply.

The pillowcase tasted terrible, but he couldn't stop biting down, grinding his teeth against the fabric as Blaine rode him toward orgasm. Grey sensed it racing toward him, but it kept rushing past, leaving him unfulfilled. He tried to shift to reach for his cock, but Blaine grabbed his hand. "No."

Grey shifted desperately, but Blaine's thighs were too strong, forcing Grey's legs apart, and refusing to let him get up on his knees. "Don't come yet," Blaine said, fucking him so hard that Grey's teeth rattled, and he had to bite the pillow again to keep from screaming.

Blaine reached around and grabbed Grey's cock. "Don't come," Blaine said.

"Blaine," Grey managed, shocked that he was even able to get the word out, but the 'please' he'd planned next came out as incoherent noises as Blaine fucked his ass with firm, rapid strokes. There was no way he wasn't going to come.

"Grey, I said don't come."

He closed his eyes and fought for control. He bit down on his lip, trying to keep from shouting, but he couldn't stop the noise after all—

Blaine slapped his ass, just as he came and the sharp shock of it exploded with the orgasm over his body. He yelled, his body jerking, as he shot his come on the sheets, and his ass squeezed Blaine's cock.

Grey moaned when Blaine pulled out, flipped him over and pushed his knees up to his chest. It was a clumsier position, but Grey was limp and his body pliable. Blaine thrust back into Grey, and Grey arched up from the stimulation. He squeezed his eyes shut, holding his breath, until Blaine lunged forward and kissed him.

Grey moaned as Blaine thrust faster and faster, reaching for his own orgasm, and when he shouted out in pleasure, Grey grabbed Blaine's ass, pulling him in tight.

If this was what being in a relationship with Blaine was going to be like. Then bring on forever.

•   •   •

GREY'S THIGHS FELT shaky when he crawled out of the bed to find his insistently ringing cell phone. When he finally located it in his pants, which had somehow ended up under the sofa cushions, he almost laughed at how rough his voice sounded when he said, "Yeah, Jamie, how's it going?"

He sat down on the couch gingerly. He hissed, realizing that he was going to be feeling Blaine's cock for days.

"What's wrong? Are you hurt? Amelia said you called in sick today, and you sound like shit. Are you okay?"

"Just fucked out, Jamie. Just fucked the fuck out."

Blaine snickered from the bed. Grey glanced over his shoulder at him and flipped him the bird.

"Oh, yeah?" Grey could almost hear Jamie's eyebrows waggling. "Is he hot?"

"He's unbelievably hot," Grey said, looking again at Blaine and continuing, "He's got the best ass I've ever fucked."

"Dammit, it's Blaine?" Jamie almost whined those words.

"Ding, ding, ding. Give the man a prize."

"Grey, you've lost your fucking mind. Don't you remember—"

"I remember a lot of things—including the fact that this is none of your fucking business." Grey passed a hand over his eyes and shook his head.

"I just don't want to see you get hurt again. But I guess it's too fucking late for that, isn't it?"

"Yeah, I think that ship sailed, Jamie."

"Christ."

There was a silence for several moments, and Grey could hear Jamie pacing on the other end of the line.

"Did Emma get the flowers?" Grey asked.

"Yeah, she loved them. I'm sure she'll call later to say thanks."

"So how was she? A genius? Born for the stage?"

"Um, no. I think she's about as born for the stage as I was, and we all know how disastrous my acting debut was."

Grey snorted in laughter. "She vomited on herself? Christ!"

"No, but she tripped on her skirt. It ripped and everyone saw her panties. I thought she'd never stop crying. Her mother wasn't the most sympathetic, either, telling her to suck it up and be tough. The only thing that made her smile the rest of the night were those fucking roses you sent."

"And that's why I'm her favorite." Grey leaned back as Blaine crossed from the bed, climbed onto his lap, and ran his hand down to cup Grey's cock. "*And* I've got to go."

"Say hi to Blaine for me."

"Will do."

"And—"

"Yeah?" Blaine kissed Grey's neck, making Grey sound a little breathless.

"I hope it works out," Jamie said before disconnecting.

Grey smiled and hung up the phone.

CHAPTER TWELVE

GREY SAT HUMMING at his desk as he reviewed the latest boards for the Amira Salons account. He thought they were just about perfect, a nip here, a tuck there, and they'd be fabulous—if he did say so himself. And of course he did.

He smiled as Amelia tripped into the room with a new set of proofs from their latest photo shoot with some young television soap stud that Grey had fucked several months prior. He'd rimmed him, fucked him, and then talked him into helping Grey with the ads for the new Polo scent for men. That account had shifted Grey and Blackburn Advertising out of the big leagues into the gigantic leagues.

"So, who is this new guy, Grey?" Amelia asked playfully. "I've never seen you so happy."

Grey rolled his eyes and took the proofs. "Get Phil or Elise in the Nashville agency on the phone for me, please. Time for my weekly long distance ass-kicking."

Amelia stopped by the door, lingered for a moment, and Grey was just getting ready to tell her to get the fuck out when she said, "Really, Grey. I've never seen you like this. It's nice." Then she tucked tail and darted away before Grey could reply.

Grey stared at the door for a moment, pursed his lips, and then finally turned his attention to the proofs.

"Well, then let's hope he sticks around for awhile," he said softly.

●　●　●

THE FIRST SEVERAL weeks flew by in a blur of sex and an incredible sensation in the depths of Grey's stomach that made him feel like he was in constant free-fall.

Blaine's body, his smile, and his laugh, invaded Grey's mind, and he could barely work. He found himself staring into space with a smile invaded Grey's mind, and he could barely work. He found himself staring into space with a smile on his lips, remembering Blaine's warm hand in his as they'd walked to the Museum of Natural History because Blaine wanted to see an exhibit on frogs.

A part of him was mortified with himself. That was the damaged boy inside, the one his father had beaten. His sullen, scared self stood guard and told him that love was bullshit, that love was a lie. It told him that he didn't do love—just fucking. Love was too dangerous and he didn't deserve it anyway.

But then the part of him that took no bullshit from anyone—even himself—would step forward and point out the obvious. It didn't matter if he didn't believe in love, he was *in* it, and if he didn't want to regret Blaine for the rest of his life, then he'd better just go with the free-fall.

So now Grey's life was Chinese food and old movies on the floor of his apartment, followed by room service and sex in Blaine's hotel suite. And sometimes it was a Broadway show followed by a late dinner and a cab ride back to Chelsea to fuck on every surface of Grey's place, just for good measure.

And when he wasn't with Blaine, touching Blaine, talking to Blaine, or listening to Blaine, he was fending off phone calls about Blaine.

"Grey, darling, I have heard the most distressing news,"

Dominique murmured petulantly. "I heard that my dear friend Mark Vanderhalder has been *dumped* by one Mr. Blaine Kellerman, who has apparently taken up residence with your cock."

Grey sighed dramatically. "Sadly, your information is bad, Dominique. Mr. Kellerman is not cohabitating with my cock, just getting fucked by it on a regular basis."

"Well, why on earth am I getting this information from Mark and not from you? Or from Blaine? I thought we were friends."

"Maybe because it's none of your business?" Grey said cheerfully. "And *maybe* because I've been too busy fucking him to take the time to inform the masses."

"Oh, you wound me, Grey. Seriously wound me." Dominique chuckled but when she spoke again, her voice was much more serious. "You realize that you've broken Mark's heart with this little affair, don't you? I tried to explain to him that you weren't the type to commit, that Blaine would be back with him momentarily, but—"

"You presume too much, Dominique," Grey muttered.

"I'm just curious what it is that you're up to. You've already got the account."

"Way too much. This isn't a conversation I'm going to have with you. My policy has always been that unless I'm sucking *your* cock, then it's none of your business."

"Oh, Grey, what I wouldn't give to have a cock for you to suck."

Grey sighed and ran a hand over his face.

But there were other phone calls, too.

"Fucking hell, Grey! What the fuck do you think you're doing?"

"Hello to you, too, Mama." Jamie hadn't gotten his potty

mouth from Cardwell or Fawn. No he'd learned cursing straight from their mother's fountain of filth. Grey had, too.

Grey leaned far back in his desk chair and braced himself for the whirlwind. He'd known it was only a matter of time before Mama was on his case about Blaine, too. He just wasn't entirely sure what angle she was going to come at, so he waited, interested to discover her line of attack.

"Did you really fucking think that I wasn't going to hear about your latest shenanigans with Blaine? Christ, breaking up the kid's fucking relationship!"

"He's not a kid, Mama," Grey sniped.

"And for what? So that you can fuck his brains out and leave him high and dry again? And don't fucking give me any, 'He left *me*' crap, because we all know which way the fucking wind blows, and it ain't up your ass."

Grey didn't say anything, just sat slumped in his chair, one hand covering his eyes.

"And what about you? Huh?" Mama went on. "How are *you* gonna fucking handle it? Because the last time you went and got your heart involved, it nearly killed you, is all I'm saying. And don't tell me you don't believe in love, 'cause, honey, you can't fucking fool me, and—"

Grey interrupted, "So who are you worried about, Mama? Blaine or me? Fuck, it's amazing that Fawn and Jamie came out of childhood relatively unscathed considering your mixed messages. God knows, I'm a mess, no thanks to you."

"I gotta tell you, Grey, I love you beyond the telling of it, but you're a fucking asshole sometimes, and you know it."

Grey snorted.

"Listen to me, jackass, all I'm saying is that if you fuck this one up, I don't know what's gonna become of you. I really don't."

Grey pulled a hand through his hair and rolled his eyes. Even so a smile tugged at the edges of his lips. "Mama, Christ! This isn't a fucking soap opera. I'm a grown man and so is Blaine and if we want to fuck each other then it's really none of your business."

Mama chomped her gum on the other end of the line finally saying, "You think I don't know you? I know you, Grey Blackburn. I know you better than you know yourself. Don't fuck up."

Then there was the most awkward phone call of all.

"Mr. Blackburn," Mark Vanderhalder sounded very different from the previous times that Grey had talked with him. "I was calling to check on the next campaign for Chill Blaine Enterprises. The one for our upcoming animated feature? I believe Madison faxed everything to you?"

"Yes, and I'm pleased to say that you'll be ready to hand over your first born to Blackburn Advertising when you see what we've worked up." Grey felt unbelievably false talking to Blaine's ex as though nothing had happened, as though he hadn't set out to take Blaine from the man and, so far, succeeded.

"Excellent. Is this something we can video conference? As you're aware," Mark's voice was decidedly bitter. "I won't be coming back to New York as originally planned. But if you need my physical presence—"

"No, we can certainly set up a video conference. That'll be no problem, Mark."

There was no way Grey wanted to bring Mark back to New York for any reason. He was just starting to feel secure with what he and Blaine were building, and it was way too soon to have the very recent ex-boyfriend on the scene. Mark no doubt had comfortable, familiar arms with which to tempt Blaine home again.

Grey closed his eyes. No, Blaine *was* home *with him*.

"Mr. Blackburn, may I ask you something?"

Fuck.

"Certainly."

"Do you love him? I mean, truly love him? The way I do?"

Grey swallowed and considered his answer. "Not the way you do. No."

Better, always, forever, beyond measure.

"Then why?"

"Because I love him the way that *I* do, and that's more information than I give most people. Goodbye, Mr. Vanderhalder."

Grey rubbed his fingertips over his eyes and took deep breaths. He'd said it out loud. But to the wrong person.

"Not you, too," Grey groaned when Fawn called.

"What? Oh, that." Fawn chuckled. "Oh, no, I'm not calling about Blaine. Although, I do want to talk to you about him."

Grey pulled out his checkbook. If it wasn't about Blaine, then it was about Reed. "How much?"

"Jesus, Grey, you'd think that all I ever do is hit you up for money for my son. I do call you for other reasons you know."

"Yes, like to bother me about Blaine. Besides, I don't mind giving it—the money, I mean."

"Well, right now you need to give a little more than money. Right now you need to give a little time."

Grey sighed and leaned back in his chair, fiddling with a pen. "All right, what'd he do now?"

"It's nothing he's done, per se, so much as the point he's at in his life. He's fourteen and he's finally really figuring out about sex, and he's confused. He's acting out."

"Confused? What's to be confused about? You like pussy?

Then you stick your cock in that. You like dick? Then you find one to suck. You like them both? Even better! More options!"

"Grey, seriously. You know it isn't as simple as that."

"So, what's he doing to act out?"

"He's dyed his hair black. And the other day he went to some piercing parlor on Church Street to get a penis piercing, but the guy wouldn't give it to him. Luckily, the owner recognized him from Mama's diner as one of her family. So he called Mama, who called Jeanine, who freaked out, and with the new baby on the way, that isn't really the best—"

"Yeah, yeah. But did he find someone to pierce his dick?"

"Grey!"

"Fawn! Get a grip!"

"I think that maybe it'd be a good idea if he visited with you for a bit. Not a long time. Just a few days. A week maybe."

"Great the kid's confused—and coming to stay with his cock-loving, ass-licking uncle is going to straighten him out, how?"

Fawn sighed. "Grey, consider it, okay? For Reed's? He needs a father right now and you're the only one he's got."

Grey sighed. He wasn't sure he was up to the task. He'd never been good with feelings. "What about Jamie? Or Caldwell?"

"They're good men and they love Reed, but he doesn't think of them as his father. That's how he thinks of *you*."

"All right. I'll figure something out." Grey sighed. "Now— am I actually going to dodge the Blaine bullet?"

"No. I only have one thing to say, though. If you love Blaine, then make it work, Grey. Jesus, no one wants to see you go down again. Everyone's rooting for you. Make it work."

CHAPTER THIRTEEN

BLAINE WAS TOO distracting to concentrate on the movie. Grey's eyes kept drifting to the left in order to admire the light from the big screen flickering over Blaine's face. Their fingers brushed together in the extra-large popcorn—Blaine had insisted on butter—and they eventually twined their slippery hands together in the depth of the almost empty bucket.

Afterwards, walking through the bright streets of Chelsea, Grey kept his arm around Blaine's shoulders, to help ward off the chill. Mark had sent some winter clothes, but no heavy coats. Grey was going to have to make Blaine buy one before long.

"After all that popcorn you ate tonight, I kept thinking I'd look over and find you'd morphed into a piglet," Grey teased, poking Blaine's side where he carried a little weight.

"Oh? Is that why you kept looking at me? I thought you were admiring my beauty."

"No such luck, Doll Face. I was trying to figure out if your nose was getting piggish or not."

"Oh ho ho, fuck you very much."

"Okay, sure, but it's your fault if we get arrested." Grey slipped around behind him, and thrust his hips into his backside, making Blaine laugh.

They walked together in contented silence for a few minutes, and when Blaine shivered, Grey asked, "Have you considered a winter coat?"

"It's a little soon, yet. Don't you think?"

Grey shrugged, wondering if maybe Blaine wasn't planning on staying for the full winter. He wrapped his arm around Blaine's shoulders, pulling him close. The warmth of his body along his side felt right, and Grey tried to think of something to say, something to convince him, something that would make Blaine want to stay.

Later, after having dinner in, and a playful fuck on the sofa, Grey asked, "Have you thought about leaving the Plaza? Maybe moving in here?"

Blaine rolled over, gazed into Grey's eyes, and kissed his lips gently. Grey's chest tightened as the seconds ticked by, until finally Blaine said again, "It's a little soon, yet. Don't you think?"

When Grey turned his head away, his heart clenching painfully, Blaine gripped his chin and forced his eyes back. "Hey, it's like fucking, remember? Don't rush it."

The next evening Grey ran his finger along the grain of his dining room table, pressed his phone to his ear, and sighed as his nephew continued ranting.

"But Uncle Grey, I wanna come live with you. I *have* to come live with you. I'm going crazy here. *Crazy*, do you understand?"

"Reed, you know that I'd love to have you come visit me, but—"

"*Crazy*, Uncle Grey! Don't you get it! Mom's making me insane! And so is Mom."

Grey sighed. It was weird that he could always tell by Reed's vocal inflection which mom he was referring to at any given moment.

"Jeanine's just a little high-strung right now. Pregnancy at her age can be—"

"Oh my *God*, you sound like Mom! She told you to say that,

didn't she? Fuck this. I'm going to go live with Uncle Jamie and Uncle Caldwell and their fifty other kids, then. And I fucking *mean* it."

Grey cradled his head in his hands and gazed across his living room at Blaine, who was sitting at the coffee table making production notes on his iPad.

"You wouldn't like it there. Caldwell's a hard ass," Grey countered. "In more ways than one."

"Uncle Grey, please. Just until Mom has the baby."

"Reed, have you really thought this through? You'd be switching schools in the middle of the year. New York's a tough town on a new kid. I just don't think it's wise. Why don't you let me work something out with your Mom? I'm sure we can come to some arrangement—"

"Fuck that!"

"Reed—"

"Fine."

Grey could just imagine the look of impotent rage on his son's face. "Can I at least come up for the week of my Christmas break, then?"

Grey glanced over at Blaine who was watching him now, his eyes curious and weighing. "Sure, buddy. That sounds great."

· · ·

"WHAT IF HE doesn't like me?" Blaine asked over dinner at the penthouse, and Grey knew just whom he was talking about.

"Everyone likes you. You're a little ray of sunshine," Grey replied, his voice honey-sweet, pinching Blaine's cheek.

Blaine batted his hand away, irritably. "The same can't be said of you."

"Because being liked is the lowest form of flattery. It's much better to be hated. Or despised. Or loathed."

Blaine picked at his food, ignoring the argument bait Grey had placed. "Really, though. What if he doesn't like me?"

Grey chewed slowly, thinking it over. "Then I guess you won't come on our annual uncle-nephew fishing trips. A great loss, I'm sure."

Blaine kicked him under the table and chuckled. "You fishing. Now that I'd pay to see."

"Then you better hope Reed likes you."

•   •   •

GREY STOOD WITH his hands on the back of the sofa in Blaine's hotel suite watching Blaine work. He was making notes rapidly as he listened to Mark on the speakerphone going over the details of the latest project that he wanted to develop, some animated movie about moles that were actually spies for Russia during the Cold War. It sounded bleak.

"It could be interesting," Blaine said. "Who do you have in mind for the main artist? And who to direct? And what's the target audience?"

"As far as directors go, I think you'd would be ideal, baby. The idea needs someone who can keep that hint of psychological violence without taking it too far."

Grey blinked at the word "baby", but Blaine seemed oblivious.

"I'll think about it. Send the script to the hotel and I'll give it a look. In the meantime, can you look around the house for that heavy coat I bought a couple of years ago in Prague?"

Mark was quiet for a moment and then replied, "I'm pretty

sure you threw that one out after it was soiled in an encounter with a, uh, hook-up."

Blaine scratched his ear, frowning. "Fuck. Yeah. I think you're right. Fuck."

"Do you want me to order a new coat for you, baby? I could have it delivered—"

Blaine met Grey's eyes, smiled and said, "No, I'll have Grey help me pick something out."

"Oh." Mark sounded as though he'd been sucker punched.

In a way, Grey thought he kind of had, and he felt a flare of anger at Blaine for toying with the man. It was cruel.

Blaine continued as if he hadn't just been a colossal dick, "Speaking of, have you been in touch with Blackburn Advertising about the new campaign for *Romeo and Juliet*?"

"Of course I have. I've got that under control."

Blaine looked to Grey and lifted his eyebrows to confirm. When Grey nodded, Blaine said his goodbyes and hung up the phone.

"Sorry about that," Blaine said seductively, rising from his chair with a sexy stretch. "But all play and no work will leave Blaine a poor boy."

Grey ran his hands down Blaine's back, and cupped his ass. "You're also a cruel tease."

"Oh, I'm not teasing," Blaine murmured, his fingers starting on Grey's belt, and his mouth pressing wet kisses to Grey's neck.

"I wasn't talking about me."

Blaine pulled back, confused. "Huh?"

"I'm talking about Mark. Stringing him along. It's not nice. If it's over, end it."

Blaine's mouth hung open and he took a step back, running a hand over his hair. "Are you *jealous*?"

"Of course not," Grey said, scowling. Who cared if that wasn't entirely true? It was entirely beside the point. "I just think you're not doing him any favors by not making it clear it's over."

Blaine tossed his hands up, and rolled his eyes, saying, "He hasn't felt my dick up his ass in well over a month, Grey, I think he's probably noticed."

Grey gritted his teeth. "Treating him like nothing's changed when it has, keeping him around like a puppy, asking him to service you at your beck and call, it's beyond unkind. It's cruel. And it's beneath you."

Blaine's eyes went bright with anger. "I'll have you know that I was more than clear that it's over. He's very well aware of that fact."

"Didn't sound like it, *baby*."

"I can't believe you're jealous of him."

Grey clenched his jaw, trying to get his temper under control. He loved Blaine, he truly did, but the way he was treating Mark was unconscionable and he wasn't going to keep silent about it. "I'm just pointing out that your behavior isn't very fucking flattering and you need to take a look at yourself. You're being a selfish prick, using and hurting the poor schmuck in the meantime." Grey frowned, a sudden cold chill shooting down his spine. "Unless I'm the poor schmuck here?"

"Fuck you. *Fuck you*." Blaine's eyes blazed.

"No, *fuck you*."

It would have felt good to slam Blaine's hotel room door behind him, but he had to be satisfied by the soft click as the hydraulic arm closed it gently.

Three hours later, the cold pavement seeping in through the soles of his shoes, and he had to admit as far as comebacks went, it'd been one of his lamest. He must be losing his edge in everything.

Pushing his hands deeper into his pockets, he kept his eyes on the pavement, remembering the glare in Blaine's eye before he'd turned his back and left the suit. And what had he done after that? He'd turned off his phone and gone off to get shit-faced. Blaine was right—Grey had always been good at games and fucking. It was relationships that he sucked at.

He should have stayed and fought it out. Or he should have gone back. Or he should have never brought up the thing with Mark to begin with, maybe. But he couldn't stand there and see Blaine acting in a way that was so completely beneath him.

Blaine was better than that.

Grey frowned. He'd been offered a blowjob in the bathroom of the bar but he hadn't accepted. Blaine gave better blowjobs than three-fourths of gay New York, hell gay USA for that matter. So why would he bother with an anonymous one? Not that what he felt for Blaine was all about sex, because—

It wasn't. Never had been.

And it sucked to be drunk when he needed to think clearly about why the doorman to his building was trying to get his attention. He'd never pegged him for gay, but he supposed that if he'd really screwed things up with Blaine, then he could fuck this guy and be done with it. Wouldn't be as good as with Blaine, but he'd at least stop thinking of the little shit for at least ten minutes and that'd be a relief.

But when he leaned in to kiss the man, he was pushed way, the doorman gasping, "What are you doing, Mr. Blackburn?"

Fuck. It'd been awhile since he'd fucked up like that.

"Shit. I'm drunk. Sorry. Just…fuck," Grey headed toward the elevator, rubbing his eyes, trying to sober up, so that he could remember what floor he lived on.

"Mr. Blackburn, I let the young man in. I hope that's all right. Usually I would never have done that, but given who he is to you, and the situation—"

Grey pressed the button to close the elevator doors without letting the man finish, and then punched the button to his floor. Blaine had come, and it would be all right. He just needed to decide what to say, how to say it. He just had to make things okay again.

The door to his penthouse was cracked and he pushed the door open, hope fluttering in his chest, ready to forgive and forget, or fuck and forget, whichever, and—

"Uncle Grey!"

CHAPTER FOURTEEN

G REY SAT ON a stool at the kitchen island opposite Reed watching him eat a peanut butter and jelly sandwich pilfered from the small cabinet of groceries that Blaine had purchased to keep at Grey's place.

"And your moms think you're at Caldwell and Jamie's," he encouraged Reed to continue.

"And Caldwell and Jamie think I'm at Phil and Denine's, and Denine thinks I'm at Mama and Roy's, and Mama and Roy think I'm at Samson's, and Samson is MIA for the weekend."

Grey nodded, trying to look sober and like he wasn't on the verge of throttling his nephew. "So, you took the bus—"

"Yeah, fucking long ride, too."

Grey took a deep, cleansing breath. It didn't help. "We need to call your mothers and tell them where you are. I hope your little ruse hasn't been discovered or everyone will be out of control with hysterics."

Reed rolled his eyes. "They oppress me."

Grey snorted. "After this little escapade, you're going to know oppression like you've never imagined, I bet." He stood and made his way toward the phone.

"Oh, and some guy's been leaving sad messages on the machine because your cell phone's off. Is he your boyfriend or something? You didn't tell me you had a boyfriend. And why do you still have a message machine? Didn't those go extinct in like nineteen ninety-nine or something?"

Grey stopped in his tracks and looked at Reed, nearly five feet ten inches tall, shaggy hair dyed black, and big hazel eyes staring at him full of questions, and with some measure of worry.

"Some guy," Grey repeated, softly, turning to the machine and almost pushing play. He thought better of it, not sure what kind of messages Blaine might have left and not wanting to subject Reed to the ridiculous fucking drama of his...Christ, his *love life*. He hated that term.

"Yeah," Reed went on. "He said that you're a son of a bitch, but that he loves you, and to call him. Then he called back and said that he was sorry and you were right. Then he called back again to say that he'd 'handled it', whatever that means. And then he called *again* and said that he wanted you to come over and make up properly. Then he called back and mentioned sucking your—"

"Enough!" Grey cradled his head in his hands; he was going to have a fucking bitch of a hangover the next morning. And why the *fuck* had he told Fawn he'd be Reed's father figure? Christ, he was clueless at this stuff.

"So is he your boyfriend?" Reed's voice held more than simple curiosity.

Grey ignored the question and pointed a finger at Reed. "I'm calling your mothers. Prepare yourself, kid. You're going to have a shitload of explaining to do."

Grey turned on his phone, both distressed and relieved to see the barrage of text messages and missed call notifications that came through. All from Blaine. Then he pressed Fawn's name on the screen and closed his eyes. He really wasn't looking forward to the coming onslaught of female hysteria.

● ● ●

REED SLEPT SOUNDLY on the sofa, sheets tucked around him, his mouth slightly open, and in the darkness Grey thought he looked ridiculously young. He made a mental note to feel Reed out about drugs and alcohol—with his family history Reed was a prime candidate for addiction.

Grey turned back to the window, looking down over the street, and saw two men walking arm and arm. He glanced at the phone in his other hand, trying to decide if he wanted to risk another nightmare phone call tonight.

The conversation with Jeanine and Fawn had been agonizing, and any adrenaline buzz that he'd had left over after the shock of finding Reed in his penthouse had been dispelled by all the shouting. Jeanine and Fawn had started out furious, passed through frightened, visited guilty, and finally, eventually, arrived at calm and resolute.

The final outcome of it all was that he, Grey Blackburn, somehow agreed to let Reed stay with him for a week, provided that Reed make up all of his school work. And he'd also agreed that Reed could return in a few weeks time to stay for the Christmas break.

"You can't reward him for this behavior, Grey," Jeanine had said.

"It isn't a reward, Jeanine," Fawn interrupted. "He needs his father."

Jeanine muttered under her breath that Grey wasn't even his father, but Fawn simply said, "He is the only father that Reed has ever known. That's all that matters now.

Jeanine had started to argue, but Grey didn't give a flying fuck what she thought. "He came all the fucking way here to see me. So, he'll see me."

"Yes, he wants to know Grey. There's no replacement for spending time with his father figure," Fawn said, her voice low.

Grey waited for another snide remark from Jeanine, but it never came.

Everyone agreed that Reed would not be taking the bus back to Nashville, though. Instead, Grey would fly down with him the following weekend.

Lastly, Reed was looking forward to three weeks of absolute grounding when he got home, as well as the wrath of two very pissed lesbian mothers, one of whom was pregnant. Part of Grey pitied his son.

Still, there was Blaine to deal with now, and it was nearly two in the morning. He checked on Reed one last time, and then retired to his bedroom, phone in hand.

It was a large room and tastefully decorated. He'd opted for something different from his loft in Music City, something more traditional, and yet it still fulfilled his requirements with regards to sensuality and simplicity.

The king-sized bed was unmade from the last romp he'd had with Blaine the prior night. He was too tired to change the sheets, so he ditched his clothes and climbed in. He could smell Blaine's shampoo on the pillow, Blaine's skin on the blanket, and the musky odor of them together all over everything—sexy and raw.

He contemplated the phone he still held in his hand and pressed Blaine's name, waiting through six rings and most of Blaine's voicemail message before hanging up. He glanced at the clock. It was late. Blaine was either asleep or had his phone turned off. Or maybe he was on a plane back to Mark and their home together in L.A., and it would be all Grey's fault.

He held the phone against his chest and closed his eyes.

. . .

BLAINE'S SKIN WAS smooth and white, gliding under his fingertips like the finest cloth. Grey pulled Blaine's back to his chest, and rolled his hips in smooth thrusts, driving his cock deeper into him. Blaine moaned and Grey opened his eyes, leaning forward to catch Blaine's expression. Blaine moved against him, encouraging him, but he was kissing someone else.

Grey adjusted his position in order to get a better look at the man they were having sex with, and felt his stomach twist at the vision of Blaine's lips moving with Mark's. They kissed and fondled one another. Grey fucked Blaine harder, trying to draw his attention away from Mark, but was rewarded only with Blaine's low halting moans that indicated he was close, and the clenching of Blaine's ass around Grey's cock as he came.

Grey's chest hurt as he clearly heard Blaine whisper "Mark" against his lover's lips.

CHAPTER FIFTEEN

GREY WOKE UP hard and terrified. He instinctively reached to his left to make sure that Blaine was there, and found the bed empty. In flashes he remembered their fight, and drinking, and—

Fuck, Reed was here.

He struggled to sit up, his head throbbing, and he didn't think it was just because of the alcohol. He slipped into his bathrobe and headed toward the bathroom. He was pretty sure he had some aspirin in there.

After his shower, Grey pulled on jeans and a white, sleeveless t-shirt, heading out to rouse his son. He'd have to deal with Blaine sometime today, too, but it was Saturday and he knew Blaine liked to sleep late.

Although, today was obviously an exception.

Grey stopped in the kitchen doorway. Reed sat at the island eating cereal that he must have found in Blaine's stash, and Blaine sat across from him idly sketching on a pad of paper.

"No fucking way. You were there when I was born?"

"Well, not *when* you were born, but not long after you were born. I met your Uncle Grey when you were just a baby."

"And, after you met Uncle Grey, that's when you met my mom? And Mama? And Uncle Jamie?"

"Right. My folks had kicked me out for being gay and I had nowhere to go. Your Uncle Grey introduced me to his family, and Mama took me in for a little while. I'm not sure Jamie liked me being there, but he was too old to be living at home anyway. And that's when he met Caldwell, so, all's well that ends well."

Reed studied Blaine carefully. "Hey, maybe I remember you, actually? You used to baby-sit for me sometimes, yeah?"

Blaine looked up from his sketch, a pleased expression on his face. "Yeah. Your mom was a good friend to me, too. I left, though, before she met your other mom. What's her name again?"

"Jeanine."

"That's right. I bet she's nice."

"She's okay." Reed waved his spoon in the air, excited now that he had placed Blaine. "I called you 'Bwaine', right? 'Cause I couldn't say the letter L until I was older."

"You were very little. I'm surprised you remember that."

Grey stood leaning against the doorframe waiting for Reed or Blaine to notice him, but Reed was fixated on Blaine, and Blaine on his paper.

"Hey, wouldn't you have been, you know, kind of *young* to be with my Uncle Grey when I was a baby?"

Blaine laughed and shrugged. "You gotta start sometime." Then he looked up sharply. "You're not thinking of starting soon are you?"

"With guys? I don't know. Maybe with girls." Reed shrugged, took a bite of cereal. "I don't know. It's weird. How do I know which one I should start with?"

Blaine smiled gently. "You'll know."

"Will I, though? Because right now I think I like both."

Grey cleared his throat and both Reed and Blaine jumped, startled to find him standing there.

"Oh, uh, hey Uncle Grey. Look who's here." Reed smiled weakly. "It's Blaine. From the messages."

Grey snorted.

Reed blushed. "How long were you listening?"

"Long enough." As Reed blushed even harder, Grey motioned to Blaine. "I need to talk to you. In the bedroom."

It was Reed's turn to snort. "Riiight. You go *talk*. Just please don't be as loud as my moms when they're making up."

Grey glared at Reed, and Blaine wrinkled his nose in disgust, murmuring "Ew," under his breath.

The door was barely shut behind them when Blaine began.

"Grey, I'm sorry. I called Mark last night and told him that he needed to move out of the house in California, get his own place, and that what we had had been good, wonderful even, but that it was also, sadly, *over*."

Grey smiled sadly. "That had to be painful for everyone."

"It was. But it's time. I know what I want and it isn't him."

"You've always gone after what you want."

Blaine put his hands on Grey's hips, going on, "I told him that if we're going to work together then there can be no more pet names and no more trying to take care of me. And no more letting me take advantage of him. I told him I'd been wrong to use him that way and I recognized it now. It was hard. The worst conversation of my life, frankly. Even worse than when I told him to stay in L.A. because I guess he knows now that there's no hope for reconciliation. But I did it. It's done. *Fin*."

"Blaine—"

"I know you're sorry for what you said last night. Let's just forget about it."

"Actually, I'm not sorry for what I said, but I shouldn't have walked out."

Blaine nodded, and Grey knew that he understood. "Though, considering who turned out to be at home waiting for me," Grey nodded toward the kitchen, "I suppose it worked out for the best." He didn't feel the need to mention stopping by the bar to get drunk, though.

Blaine's hands rubbed up and down Grey's arms, and he looked over his shoulder as though he could see through the walls, before asking, "What's he doing here? I thought he wasn't coming for a few more weeks?"

"Apparently, Reed got creative with his babysitting money and bought a bus ticket."

Blaine's eyebrows shot up. "Wow."

"Yeah."

Blaine frowned, searching out Grey's eyes. "So, why?"

"I don't know yet. I'm waiting for the other shoe to drop. Although that may have been it in the kitchen. Sexual identity crisis." Grey covered his face with one hand. "Christ. What the fuck was I thinking agreeing to be his dad?"

Blaine wrapped his arms around Grey's waist, and said, "He's just young. Give him another—"

"Few years? He'll be twenty before we know it. The same age you were when I fucked you blind the first time."

Blaine rose on his toes and pressed a kiss to Grey's lips, then rubbed his nose against Grey's. "Thank God the blindness wasn't permanent. It would've really fucked with my job as a film producer."

"There's always next time," Grey threatened, leaning down to kiss Blaine's lush lips.

* * *

"WELL, THAT WAS a lot quieter than my moms. Thanks," Reed said, still shoveling cereal into his mouth, and reading an old copy of OUT magazine that he'd found somewhere.

Grey sat down next to his son and said, "So, what do you want to do while you're here? Since this is an unscheduled visit, you do realize you're going to be spending a lot of time in my office, right?"

Reed lifted his shoulders dismissively. "Anything is better than listening to Mom bitch at me about my hair." He looked up in excitement and grabbed Grey's arm. "The one thing I really, really want, though, is a Prince Albert piercing. I already looked into the perfect place to get it done, but I have to get a guardian's written permission. Come on, Uncle Grey—"

"What? You think I have a death wish? Not on your fucking life, kid. Your moms would cut my balls off."

Reed narrowed his eyes, withdrew his hand, and said around a mouthful of cereal, "Fine, I'll find someone else to do it and they might not have clean instruments. I could get an infection and my dick will rot off, and it'll be your fault because you wouldn't give me permission to get it done someplace clean and decent!"

Grey rolled his eyes.

Blaine leaned on the kitchen island across from them, put his chin in his hand, and mused, "Such a drama queen. Like uncle, like nephew."

Grey flipped him off.

The next day, Grey stood with his hands in his pockets, his shoulders hunched, and his lip between his teeth. The tattoo-covered, needle-wielding owner of New York Adorned guided Grey's shirtless son into a chair, asking, "So, right or left?"

Blaine, examining the walls of possible tattoo art, volunteered, "I got my right side done."

Grey glared at him. He considered it mainly Blaine's fault

that they were even here. Blaine was the one who'd told Reed all about his own piercing, long gone and the hole grown over now. Saying things like, "No it didn't hurt too much", and "You could always take it out if you don't like it," and "It's a lot less dangerous than a Prince Albert."

Inspired, Reed had become more and more adamant, throwing the potential health risks of him getting a friend to do it when he got back to Nashville in Grey's face until he'd finally agreed to supervise the damn thing.

Reed nodded at the piercer. "Right."

Grey felt a little queasy as the man brought the piercing needle to Reed's chest. He bit down harder on his lip, and then felt a tug on his arm. Blaine pulled him sideways, indicating something on the wall. "What do you think of me getting this on my ass?"

It was a small black tribal design of some sort and Grey was about to make a derisive comment about defiling the pristine beauty of Blaine's globes, when he was distracted by Reed's sudden yelp of pain.

Turning back to his nephew, he met wide, hazel eyes, hot with excitement.

"Cool. So cool," Reed said, laughing and grimacing at the same time.

Blaine grinned and agreed. "Yeah. It looks good, Reed."

Reed's eyes were luminescent with joy when he said, "Thanks, Uncle Grey."

Grey smiled shakily. He was so fucking dead. Jeanine would eat one of his balls for breakfast over this, and Fawn would eat the other.

Blaine whispered in his ear, "Now you'll be the cool uncle for the rest of his life."

"Great. Because that was what I was aiming for," Grey muttered sarcastically.

Blaine laughed and kissed his cheek before going over to congratulate Reed on his gold-pierced nipple.

That night, alone together in the apartment after Blaine had returned to his hotel room, Reed had questions.

"Do you like it when he fucks you?" Reed asked, seriously, muting the television and turning to Grey with big eyes. "Does it hurt?"

Grey had been relieved that Reed seemed to get along so well with his lover. Although, he supposed he shouldn't have been too surprised. Reed had always liked Blaine, even as a baby. Still, it gave him hope that maybe his thoughts of a long-term future weren't too ridiculous—no matter how fucking crazy it felt for him to be considering such things.

Grey thought hard before answering Reed's question. The light from the television flickered across Reed's face, his lips drawn taut with anxiety. "I don't mind answering your questions, kiddo, but do you mind if I ask some of my own?"

Reed looked away, shrugging with some show of discomfort. "I guess not. I don't know. Maybe."

Grey wanted to pull him close, tuck him under his arm, and kiss his soft hair, the way he had when Reed was young.

Instead, Grey smoothed sweaty palms down his jeans, and sat forward on the couch, gazing down at Reed on the opposite end. "It's okay if you're gay, Reed, and it's okay if you're straight. It's also okay if you're bisexual. Or asexual. We're going to love you no matter what."

Reed lowered his eyes and asked softly, "Is it gross? Is it gross to suck cock? The guys at school all say it is. They called me a faggot. When I didn't get mad about it, they said it proved I'm a queer." Reed kept his eyes averted. "Am I? Do you know, Uncle

Grey?"

Grey lowered his head, deciding to take it one step at a time. "I don't think it's gross to suck cock, Reed. But some people do. Hell, some straight girls think it's gross. Sex is highly personal. People like different things. It's okay to not like something that someone else thinks is fucking amazing, and it's okay to like something that another person thinks is gross. It's like how people have different favorite colors. It shouldn't be a big deal."

Reed lifted a brow at the analogy, but remained silent.

"As for guys at school saying it's bad to suck cock, there'll be a day when people don't say those things anymore. I hope you live to see it. I probably won't." Grey smiled sadly. "But, the other thing is, fuck 'em, you know? If you like the idea of sucking cock, then who cares what they think? Fuck 'em."

"I care what they think."

Grey took a deep breath. He could remember the pain of being different at fourteen—of wanting to fuck guys, of having a father who beat him, of having to avoid the prying eyes and taunting remarks. He remembered wishing that he could just fit in.

But then Grey started working on the walls that had become his defense, and his prison, for the rest of his life. He didn't want Reed to end up in the same trap, but he didn't want him letting other people tell him how to live his life, either.

"I know you do," he said softly. "It's normal to care what they think. So, why didn't you get mad when they called you a faggot?"

Reed straightened his shoulders and put his chin up. "Most of the men I know are faggots and I love them. It's not an insult to me. That's what I said. I said, 'Whatever. That's not an insult to me.'"

Grey nodded and waited a few seconds.

"But, Uncle Grey—" Reed bit his lip and looked away. "Uncle Grey, I lied. I don't know—I mean, I don't want to be—what if I am—and people hate me and—"

"It's still not an easy world to be queer in, kiddo."

"I was faking it. I felt so scared when they said that. And when I told them—" Reed didn't meet his eye, his voice lowering to a whisper. "I was ashamed. I was embarrassed, Uncle Grey. I pretended that I wasn't, but I was, and now I'm scared that they're right, and that I'm a fag, too. What if I am?"

Grey sat in silence, completely out of his depth. He was tempted to blaze ahead with his usual quips that he'd perfected over time, with comments like, "Fuck them all," but he bit back the habits of years because this was his *son*, not Jamie, and Grey was forty-three, not fifteen. Even if he felt catapulted back in time at the moment, to the point that he could smell the locker room, see his gym teacher naked and soapy, sense the steam from the showers, and feel the pounding of his own beating heart.

"Uncle Grey?"

Grey cleared his throat. "I can't answer the question for you, Reed. I don't know whether or not you're gay or straight. Only you can answer that."

"Sometimes I think about girls," Reed volunteered. "And I get excited, you know? But I've thought about certain guys, too, and the same thing happens. I get hard. Is that normal? Does that mean I'm just a huge slut or something? What if I just want to fuck everyone?"

Grey tried to stifle his smile. He could just imagine Blaine's comment if he were here. Like uncle, like nephew, indeed.

"Only time will tell, Reed. Lots of people are attracted to both sexes. It's called being bisexual."

"Did you ever fuck a girl?"

Grey nodded, looking down at his hands. "It wasn't my bag."

Reed nodded. "What about Blaine? Did he ever fuck a girl?"

"You'll have to talk to Blaine about that."

"My gay pal Keegan said that he fucked a girl once and that it was the most disgusting thing he's ever done, even grosser than dissecting frogs in ninth grade."

Grey lifted his brows, stuck out his lower lip, and tried to look bemused, and not amused.

Reed continued, "But another guy at school said that if you butt fuck someone then you get shit on your dick, and that's gross, too. I mean, shit's gross, right?"

Grey pursed his lips and wished to God for the right words because he was so far out of his depth with this one. Though, he knew now why Reed hadn't been willing to discuss any of this stuff with Fawn and Jeanine. He could only imagine their reaction to the idea of shit on dicks.

"Well, Reed, sex is always messy—" Grey ran a hand through his hair. "And, there are things you can do to…prepare. Do you plan to test this out? I can be as graphic as you need, but I have to know what you want here." Grey went for broke. "Kiddo, do you need me to tell you about ass-fucking, condoms, lube, and the whole works?"

Reed fiddled with the television remote control, his cheeks turning red. Finally he pressed the power button and the room plunged into darkness. "I looked it up online, but I don't know if I can trust what I read. Yeah, tell me how to do it, Uncle Grey. In case I want to try it out."

Grey's mouth went dry, and for the first time in more years than he wanted to count he was embarrassed at the idea of discussing sex.

But he reached over, flipped on another lamp so that he could watch for Reed's reactions, cleared his throat, and launched into a detailed description of anal sex and the accompanying preparations.

His own cheeks burned but he was Reed's father figure. He'd made Fawn that promise, and sentenced the poor kid to a life with an absentee messed up uncle-father and two rug-munching moms.

He owed the kid at least this much.

CHAPTER SIXTEEN

TWINING HIS FINGERS in Blaine's hair, Grey stared up at the ceiling. Blaine was fast asleep on Grey's chest, worn out from a busy day, and from a romp in the shower before bed. Reed was down the hall, supposedly asleep, but Grey suspected that he was playing games on the computer, or, fuck, maybe even watching porn again.

Grey ran his fingertips over his eyes, remembering earlier, after dinner, when he and Blaine had been sitting quietly in the living room working on separate projects. Reed had bounded out of his bedroom, racing down the hall to inform them that the tests were inconclusive; he'd had good orgasms from watching guy-on-guy, girl-on-girl, and guy-on-girl porn.

Blaine had struggled not to laugh hysterically, but the hand over his mouth, and his watering eyes had pretty much given him away.

Grey was glad to have a good enough relationship with Reed that they could discuss sex to some extent, but he'd been completely silenced at Reed's announcement, unsure of where to even begin.

Eventually, Reed had said, "I think I might just be a slut."

Blaine had excused himself at that point, his shoulders shaking violently, as he tore out of the den towards Grey's bedroom.

Then Grey and Reed had a long discussion about the dangers of online porn—entirely hypocritical on Grey's part—and he hoped he'd at least turned the kid away from the seedier sites.

Grey rubbed a lock of Blaine's hair between his fingers, and then flipped out the bedside lamp. Maneuvering Blaine slightly to curl up around him, he settled in for sleep. He wondered how long he needed to wait before he could ask Blaine to move in with him.

If relationships were just like fucking, it seemed like they'd been fucking long enough by now, surely. But what did he know?

He guessed he'd have to gird his loins and find out.

*   *   *

AS THE TAXI pulled up to take them to the airport, Reed hugged Blaine goodbye, and Grey wrapped his arm around Blaine's neck, pulled him close and kissed his forehead.

"Sure you don't want to come with us, Doll Face? I know Mama would be thrilled to see you."

Blaine shook his head. "Next time. I've got some things I have to handle here this weekend. Call me when you get to Jeanine and Fawn's." Blaine pushed up on his tiptoes and kissed Grey's lips gently, whispering, "You should fuck some hot guys at Tribe for me. You know, for old-times sake."

"I don't want to fuck any guy but you."

Blaine's smile was radiant. "Oh, really?"

"Really."

Reed stuck his head out of the taxi. "We'll miss the plane! Come on, Uncle Grey!"

Grey left Blaine behind on the sidewalk, his heart swelling at the giant smile lingering on Blaine's face. It was only once he was on the plane that he realized Blaine hadn't returned the monogamy sentiment.

Fawn, dressed in blue jeans and a sweater that showed off her tits, picked them up at the airport, hugged and kissed them both, and then said to Reed, "You're in for a hell of a grounding. You know that, right?"

Reed shrugged in acknowledgement but said nothing.

"I'm just warning you. Jeanine is still very angry about you taking off like that." She shoved blond hair behind her ear and gazed at her son with serious, brown eyes. "What if something had happened to you, Reed? It was very irresponsible."

"I got a nipple ring," Reed announced, lifting up his shirt. "Guess you'll have to throw in some time for that, too."

Fawn gasped, turned to Grey and whapped him on the arm. "Grey! What were you thinking?"

"I was thinking that my nephew wanted a dick piercing and a nipple ring seemed harmless in comparison," Grey said casually, dreading the explosion when Jeanine found out.

"Yeah," Reed said enthusiastically. "Blaine and Uncle Grey took me to a really good place in New York to have it done. Totally clean, Mom. It kicked ass."

Fawn smiled tightly. "I see. Well, let's hurry up." She stalked ahead muttering, "Let's get home and get this over with."

Nashville was always…well, Nashville. It never changed. The dreary buildings and familiar roads still clung a little too tightly too him. Grey shifted in his seat, tugging at his seatbelt, trying not to let the city unsettle him.

As they approached the turn to Jeanine and Fawn's street, Reed grew more and more sullen. Grey reached over to massage his neck in sympathy. "It'll be okay. You'll see."

Reed made a non-committal noise and turned to look out the window.

Grey drew his hand away, sighing. He understood. Nashville

made him feel trapped too. He already missed New York—and Blaine.

*   *   *

JAMIE'S HOUSE HAD always been highly organized, a well-run machine. But when Grey walked into the living room with a still-smarting Reed on his heels, he found Matthew and Jarrod, Jamie and Caldwell's newest foster kids, making a fort out of old boxes and blankets.

He just shook his head, noting that time, and kids, changed everything.

"Reed!" Matthew shouted, running toward him at full-tilt. The six year old was the oldest of the two children, and Jarrod's natural brother. Their mother had been a meth addict and abusive. When she lost custody of the boys, there'd been no family to speak of to take them in, and they'd been relegated to the foster system.

Caldwell and Jamie had applied to be their foster parents, but they'd been completely shocked when they'd been awarded the children. After all, despite Jarrod's problem with toilet training (something the psychologists chalked up to neglect and probable sexual abuse), the two boys were both young, in good health, and generally easy to place.

Still, Child and Family Services decided that Caldwell and Jamie were a good fit based on their past history with foster kids—and Jamie's huge heart and reputation in the foster community didn't hurt, either.

"Reed, gonna babysit?" Jarrod asked, coming over more slow-ly, obviously wary of Grey.

"Maybe," Reed said, raising a brow and crossing his arms over his chest. "Depends on how much they pay me."

"Emma babysat us yesterday while Jamie and Caldwell went to Costco," Matthew said, sliding his arm around Reed's waist and clinging to him. "She made us cookies."

"Emma's too little to babysit," Reed said, frowning. "She's only eleven."

"She's big enough for half an hour or so. I had my cell phone," Jamie said, coming out of his kitchen with a grin on his face.

Grey hugged him tightly, breathing in Jamie's unique smell, then kissed his cheek.

"I'm telling Caldwell you kissed that man," Matthew said, still hugging Reed.

Jamie laughed, and gently cuffed the kid. "You are, huh? You go right ahead, mister. And *that man* is Uncle Grey to you."

"Emma's Uncle Grey?" Jarrod asked, his eyes lighting with interest and turning to measure Grey more thoroughly.

"And *my* Uncle Grey," Reed said, carefully dislodging Matthew's arms. He looked up at Jamie saying, "I'll watch them. Go talk." He waved toward the kitchen. "Hey, squirt." Reed grabbed Jarrod around the waist and hung him upside down. "Ugh, you're getting too big for this." He dropped him to the ground again, and moved toward the fort. "What're you guys building?"

Grey followed Jamie to the kitchen where the magic happened and pies were cooling on the counter. As the door closed behind them, he said, "Christ Jamie—"

"I know, I know." Jamie waved his hands at Grey. "Don't get started."

Grey pulled Jamie close and hugged him again. It'd been a while since he'd seen him and the comfort of Jamie's scent made his heart slow in his chest, and his breaths grow more regular. He hadn't realized that he was so wired until he felt himself unwinding in Jamie's embrace. Memories of the years they'd shared a room welled up inside him. Something about Jamie, even more than Fawn, always made him feel like he was home.

Releasing Jamie from the hug, he sat down at the table and motioned toward the pies. "Gonna feed me?"

"No."

"Why are you so cruel?"

"They have to cool first. You can have some later." Then Jamie settled in next to him, talking a mile a minute about his foster kids, their cousin Samson's law school studies, Caldwell's latest promotion, Jeanine's pregnancy, and Emma being too pretty for her own good—he was already having to ward off boys who were sniffing around her.

"What about you?" Jamie asked, finally.

"Oh, you know, the same as ever. Fabulous life, fabulous fucking, fabulous city, fabulous job. The usual."

Jamie rolled his eyes. "What about *Blaine*?"

Grey shrugged, not meeting Jamie's eyes. He was pissed as hell to feel a small smile forming on his lips.

"Shit, you're over the fucking moon for him. You always were. Just tell me it's mutual." Jamie sighed.

"It's mutual, Jamie," Grey said softly, still not looking at his brother, and feeling warmth spread through him at the memory of Blaine's kiss by the taxi. Though a chill passed over him again when he remembered that Blaine hadn't returned his declaration of monogamous intent.

"So, why didn't he come with you? Mama's gonna be pissed as hell. She wanted to see him."

"He said next time. He had some business to attend to. Not everyone is as happy with their small fortune as you are, Jamie."

"Like Caldwell says, 'Who needs more than we've got?'"

Grey nodded, kissing Jamie's forehead. He actually understood. Grey had money, power, a summer home in Italy, an unbelievably successful advertising firm, a pseudo-son to be proud of, and Blaine.

For the first time in his entire life, he thought he might have a concept of 'enough'. What more could he possibly want?

Later that night, tucked into the guest bed at Jeanine and Fawn's house, Grey rolled onto his side and listened to the dead silence all around him. How the fuck could people stand to sleep in all this quiet?

He reached out to the cell phone on the nightstand and resisted the urge to call Blaine again. He'd called twice already—once when they first got off the plane, and once after dinner, but it had gone straight to voice mail both times.

He didn't know when he'd become a Jewish mother, but visions of Blaine passed out in his hotel suite, overdosing on some drug, choking on his own vomit filled his mind. Which was ridiculous since, as far as he knew, Blaine didn't use drugs.

Or Blaine being hit by a car, in an ambulance to a hospital, unconscious from his injuries, and no one knew to call him. Fuck, he was going insane. It had only been about fifteen hours since he'd seen Blaine. He was being fucking ridiculous.

He should've forced Jamie to go dancing with him at Tribe—well, now it was called Castle, or some shit like that—just to get his mind off Blaine. But he'd let Jamie get out of it claiming fatherhood and Caldwell as his excuses.

Grey had sat through dinner with Fawn, a very pregnant Jeanine, and Reed, and then he'd actually headed to bed at eleven o'clock, like some old man. He imagined Blaine was out at the clubs in New York dancing his heart out, and, given that no promise had been made between them, possibly fucking his brains out, too. He suddenly wondered why he and Blaine had never gone to clubs in New York together when that had been a big part of their relationship when they'd been younger.

But he didn't really want to go to clubs with Blaine—or go to clubs at all. Sure, in the past he'd often headed out to places like that for an anonymous fuck, but Grindr had alleviated the need to do that.

Besides, he was—as much as he hated to admit it—too old. He was forty-three and going out clubbing wasn't on his agenda anymore. At his age, he'd look like a twat if he was out on the prowl every night. There came a point when it just wasn't dignified for a man to try to stay in that scene. He was glad he'd known when it was time to get out.

But Blaine was still young enough, only thirty-four, wealthy, and so beautiful. No doubt he'd get a lot of ass tonight if he wanted it.

Grey flopped onto his back, stomach twisting, sweating through the mental images of Blaine fucking anonymous asses and mouths all night long.

Fuck. He had to admit it. He was jealous.

CHAPTER SEVENTEEN

"**U**NCLE GREY, WILL you buy me something?" Emma asked over breakfast, her big, brown eyes pleading.

"Emma, that's not polite," Jamie said, shaking his head then leaning over to butter Jarrod's biscuit for him, despite his death glare.

"Sure, Emmycakes," Grey said, whapping the back of Emma's head affectionately. "What do you want? A nipple ring?"

"That's not funny, Grey," Jamie threatened, brandishing his butter knife at him. "Not funny at all."

"I'm not taking it out," Reed said, darkly, frowning into his milk. Grey had liberated him from his mothers' house again that morning for breakfast with Caldwell and Jamie. But Reed was still pouting about the terms of his grounding. "I don't care what the moms say. I don't care how long they punish me. I'm not taking it out."

Caldwell rolled his eyes, took a deep breath and a huge bite of biscuit. His handsome face quivered with pleasure as he chewed and swallowed. "Damn good biscuit, sweetheart," he said to Jamie, who preened like a nineteen fifties housewife.

"No, not a nipple ring." Emma laughed. "Reed is weird. No, I want a necklace that I saw at the mall. It has two bright blue stars at the bottom, and a red heart in between, and it'll look perfect with my new dress that I got. Please Uncle Grey?"

"Emma, Jamie told you it isn't polite to ask Grey for things,"

Caldwell intoned seriously, his slim lips going flat with disapproval. "We discussed this. You have your own money—"

Reed interrupted, "And your own fathers—"

"—to buy things with," Caldwell droned on.

"That's why we give you an allowance," Jamie added as backup.

"But Mom took that money for groceries," Emma said.

Jamie looked to Caldwell, and their eyes spoke volumes.

"Whatever Jitterbug wants, Jitterbug gets," Grey said, cheerfully, hoping to take the focus off Emma's situation. He trusted Caldwell and Jamie to get a handle on that pronto. His cell phone rang and he fumbled in his pocket for it, disappointed that the caller ID revealed that it was just Fawn. He sent it to voicemail.

"By the way," Jamie said, turning to him when his eye-conversation with Caldwell was over. "Mama's pissed as hell that you haven't come to see her. You'd better get your ass over there before she has an aneurysm."

"Mama would stroke out? On account of little old me? I'm flattered."

"Get over there. Today."

After breakfast was over and he'd returned Reed to his mothers' clutches, Grey drove to the diner. Sitting in the parking lot before going in, he called Blaine—irritated when it went straight to voice mail yet again.

Inside, his scrawny mama clung to Grey with a strength he'd forgotten she contained. He stooped so she didn't have to reach up so far, holding her gently, as she tried to squeeze the life out of him. When he finally tried to straighten, thinking that she'd break her hold when he stood up, she stayed attached to his neck, and her feet dangled a few inches from the ground.

"Christ, are you losing weight again, Mama? What will Roy have to hold on to at night if you keep this up?" he asked, finally managing to pry her hands free.

Mama cracked her gum at him, her grey eyes shining happily. "Everybody, this is my other baby!" Mama announced to the diner, which was full of an assortment of people that Grey didn't recognize.

A virtual stable full of new asses to cruise.

Yes, the time when he'd been the king slut of Church Street was long gone, and only a few faces in the crowd seemed to register who he was. Grey suspected it was more likely due to his interviews in *Out* and other gay magazines as a queer businessman than to his escapades in Nashville's backrooms.

Grey sat at the counter and ordered a coffee, feeling not quite comfortable in a place that used to be his second home. Time can make even the smallest difference feel exaggerated sometimes, and the new waiters, the new linoleum on the floor, and the computer to ring up orders bothered him.

"So, Grey, tell me about Blaine," Mama said, waggling her eyebrows. "I hear you're hot and heavy again. You two never could keep your hands off each other."

"What's to tell? It sounds like Jamie's told you everything anyway." Grey sipped his coffee and consulted his cell phone. There were no new messages.

"So ten years apart and true love conquers all?"

"Yes, it's quite romantic," Grey agreed. "I guess I'm proof that when your prince charming comes along, anyone can have a dysfunctional love affair that spans decades."

Mama rolled her eyes and stuck her tongue in her cheek.

The cell phone in his hand vibrated, and, checking the caller ID, he slid off the stool. "I've got to take this call."

He was barely out of the diner when he said, "Where the fuck have you been?"

"Hi. I love you, too."

"Where are you?"

Blaine sighed. "I'm in L.A."

"What? Why?"

"It's a long story, but Mark told me *last week* that the contracts with Sony for the new feature needed to be signed in person this *Wednesday* and I was gonna fly out Tuesday—you know, to kiss some respective ass." Blaine sighed. "But then Mark called *yesterday* and said he'd fucked up and the meetings are *tomorrow.* Because I'm completely unprepared for the presentation, and because I have to schmooze the execs from Sony, I had to cut out of New York last night."

"Sounds like someone's balls need to be in a sling."

Blaine snorted. "Yeah, and not just for that, either. Mark hasn't had time to really leave the house yet, you know, and he flipped out when Scott came over last night."

Grey was silent, not entirely following. Everyone knew that the sexy actor Scott Alpine and Blaine were old friends—there'd been a lot of gossip about the two of them hooking up around the time Blaine's first movie had come out. At the time Grey had been insanely jealous.

Blaine continued, "I had to fucking remind him that I was in town for *work* that he'd insisted I come in for, that I'd rather be with you, and that what I was doing with Scott was none of his business anymore. But then I got pissed when I realized that I was fucking explaining myself to him and hurting him more—"

"Wait, I'm not sure I'm following you. You left New York yesterday, hopped a plane to L.A., met up with your old friend Scott Alpine, and fought with your ex-boyfriend about it, but you didn't have time to fucking call me back?"

"It was late. But I totally should have called." Blaine lowered his voice and Grey heard someone talking in the background. "Maybe I shouldn't have invited Scott over, not with our extensive history. It was bound to upset Mark, but I wasn't thinking about that at all. I've already apologized to him for hurting him, making that mistake, and I sent Scott home."

Grey didn't know what to say, finally swallowing around his suddenly thick tongue, to ask, "Your extensive history?"

"Huh? Oh, yeah. Hold on." Blaine said loudly, "Mark! I'm going to step out back, don't eat all the Pad Thai, okay?"

Grey walked around the corner of the diner, his mind whirring. He felt like he'd been sucker punched. Apparently, Blaine was good at doing that to people.

"Yeah, well, obviously nothing happened last night. Not with Mark upset and everything else besides. But Scott and I have been fuck buddies for years. I just assumed Mark would already be staying in a hotel while he looked for a new place. So when I arrived with Scott, and Mark saw him—" Blaine groaned.

Grey couldn't think, his heart was thrashing in his chest, and he couldn't breathe right. Why had Scott been with Blaine anyway? Were they going to fuck had Mark not been there? He knew he should ask those questions, but he didn't want to know the answer. His heart felt like it might die in his chest. He finally mumbled, "I've got to go. Later."

He disconnected the call and leaned against the side of the building, bent at the waist, his hands on his knees. He tried to catch his breath while his cell phone rang again and again in his pocket.

Love was pain. He'd learned that once. How had he forgotten? What on earth made him think love was worth this vulnerable, consuming fear of loss? His stomach hurt and he slid to the sidewalk, a queen overdosing on his own drama for all of Church Street to see.

• • •

GREY SAT ON the front swing of Fawn and Jeanine's house smoking his first cigarette in over a year. The nicotine was making him feel shaky. He knew that he didn't really need to be pumping himself full of chemicals, but he couldn't think of anything better to do with his hands or mouth.

At last count, he had ten voicemail messages and seventeen texts, but he'd refused to check them. He couldn't talk to Blaine, or listen to anything he had to say, until he'd worked out what he was feeling, until he understood what was choking him.

He knew what Mama would say. She'd call it the green-eyed monster, and he knew she'd be right, but why? Why was he feeling this when he'd never been one to get hung up on monogamy?

Besides, they'd never laid any ground rules for their relationship, and he knew without a doubt that Blaine was emotionally invested in him, but *what was happening*? Why was Blaine in L.A. instead of in Music City with him? And why the fuck did Grey care?

He came to a scary conclusion. It was because this was so new, so fresh to him. This desire to build a life with someone was a revelation. And he'd just gotten Blaine back after too many years.

And Blaine had walked away from Mark so easily after all their time together. How invested could he really be in Grey now? How little would it take for him to think that the weather looked better from someone else's windows? Scott Alpine's for example.

The front door creaked open, and Grey looked up, expecting to see Fawn.

"Uncle Grey?"

"Hey, kiddo," Grey said softly, taking another drag from his cigarette. "Isn't it kind of late? Shouldn't you be asleep?"

Reed joined him, his tall frame, almost as tall as Grey himself, curled up on the swing, tucking his feet underneath him. He watched Grey intently in the dark, shoving shaggy, black hair out of his eyes.

"Blaine texted me tonight," Reed said with deliberate nonchalance that Grey recognized as his own.

"Yeah?"

"Yeah. He was looking for you."

"Mmm," Grey replied, staring at the streetlight down the road, noting the way the bugs flitted about underneath it, drawn to the light.

"I don't know why, but I lied and told him you were out with Uncle Jamie."

Grey nodded, flicked his cigarette ash, and kicked back in the swing with a sigh.

Reed went on, "Anyway, it just seemed like you wouldn't want him to know that you're moping out here on the porch."

Grey snorted.

"He said he'd call you in the morning. It's hard to tell by text, but he sounded upset, too. I don't know what's going on, but...yeah."

Grey chewed on his lip, then took another draw from the cigarette, closed his eyes and thought over the phone call again. Blaine hadn't sounded at all like he was concerned about Grey's reaction. He'd been almost conspiratorial in his tone, as though he'd expected Grey to champion him flying across the country and meeting up with Scott Alpine—mega-star and regular fuck buddy.

And Grey knew there was a time when he would have said, "Good for you, Doll Face. Go fuck his brains out." But now was not that time. Instead he'd had a panic attack and run away like a child.

"Are you going to call him?" Reed asked. He sounded nervous, and Grey finally looked at him again, saw that he was scared, and touched his cheek gently.

"Yeah. I'll call him."

"I like Blaine. He makes you happy. I've never seen you happy until him."

"I like him, too." Grey smiled a little, stubbed out his cigarette and stood into a full stretch. "Let's go to bed now, all right? Your moms will kill me if they find us out here this late."

Reed almost didn't fit under Grey's arm, he'd grown so tall. When they reached the top of the stairs, Grey pulled him close and kissed his forehead.

"It'll be all right. Sleep tight."

Then he went back to his room and read through all the texts Blaine had sent staring at one in particular:

It's like fucking, remember? Don't pull out before the big finish.

He replied with an apology for being unresponsive and a promise to talk in the morning. And then he powered his phone off for the night.

．　．　．

WHEN GREY REACHED the bottom of the stairs the next morning, Reed was on the floor of the living room wrestling with the neighbor's big dog. He rolled around with it, laughing, and grunting, and the dog let out a loud, playful bark.

"Hey, hey, hey," Fawn called from the kitchen. "Knock it off. You'll wake Grey."

"It's too late," Grey said, striding across the room to collect his jacket from the sofa. "I'm already awake. And I'm headed off to the diner. Want to go, Reed?"

Fawn appeared in the doorway from the kitchen, wiping her hands on a dish cloth.

"Can I, Mom?" Reed asked, pushing the dog away and standing up to gaze hopefully at his mother with wide his eyes. Grey smirked, knowing that Fawn would cave.

"Well, you know you're still grounded, Reed, but so long as Uncle Grey is with you, then I guess you can go. Just take Humphrey back to the neighbor's house."

Reed let the dog back outside and then dashed past Grey, up the stairs, saying, "Let me get my jacket!"

Fawn turned to him, lifted her finger in warning and said, "But no piercings or tattoos, Grey. Understand me? I want him back in pristine condition."

Grey turned to yell up to Reed. "Hurry up, kiddo! That tattoo artist won't wait all day!"

"Where are you going exactly?" Fawn asked, pushing hair out of her eyes and checking her watch. "Jeanine will want him home by dinner."

"Just to the diner, like I said. I'm meeting Jamie, Caldwell, and some of the old gang there." While he kept up with Jamie and Caldwell, he hadn't really talked to his old friend Doug or his lover Ramon in years. They'd been more casual friends than anything else, but, Grey was willing to admit he'd missed them.

"Oh, yeah? I haven't seen those guys in so long," Fawn said

with a hint of sadness. "Tell Doug and Ramon hi from me."

The gang, as Jamie referred to their mutual friends, minus the darkly handsome Ramon, was in a booth and in the midst of heavy gossip when Grey and Reed walked in. They sat with their heads together looking at something Doug had up on his phone.

"What's this?" Grey asked, trying to grab the phone out of Doug's hands.

"Nothing," Doug smiled, tucking it under the table. "Just some celebrity titillation. Stuff that only silly queens like me get excited about."

Doug sounded nervous, and Jamie and Caldwell weren't meeting his eye, but Grey let it drop, assuming it was something that wasn't appropriate for Reed's eyes. God only knew what they'd been looking at, probably pictures of a celebrity's cock, caught at a nude beach in France.

Grey slid in next to Doug, and Reed next to Caldwell and Jamie. "Sorry that Ramon couldn't make it," Doug said. "He had to report in to work at the airport. Someone called in sick."

"Give him my best," Grey said politely.

Then everyone's attention turned to Reed. Doug reached across to touch Reed's dyed hair and ask questions about the product he'd used. Jamie and Caldwell sat snuggled together, smiling in amusement as Reed talked about convincing his friend to dye his hair, and the tattoo he was going to get when he turned eighteen.

Then Reed lifted his shirt. "Look what Uncle Grey and Blaine got for me!"

"Christ Grey!" Jamie exclaimed. "What the hell were you thinking? Did Jeanine chew you a new one, or what?"

"Ate one of my balls for breakfast, actually," Grey muttered, signaling for coffee.

"Blaine's the best," Reed went on. "He told me all about having sex with a girl. He said that it wasn't as gross as some people say. He said it felt good."

Doug pursed his lips and batted his eyes. "Well, if you like to give it then I guess any nice, tight spot will do. But if you're a big old nelly bottom like me, well, girls—they just don't have the equipment, if you know what I mean. And I think you do."

Reed laughed.

Caldwell said, "Now let's keep it clean, guys. Reed is still just fourteen."

"You don't have to keep it clean," Reed contradicted. "I've watched porn. I know what happens."

Grey closed his eyes and shook his head, bringing his thumb and forefinger to the bridge of his nose.

"Grey, don't tell me you let him—"

"Yes, Jamie, I took him to a sex club in New York," Grey said, exasperated. When Jamie blanched, Grey continued, "What the fuck? Of course I didn't!"

"There are sex clubs in New York? Can I go?" Reed looked like he might actually beg.

"No!" Grey said, sipping his coffee and running his hand through his hair. "Just…no."

Doug's cell started to ring, and he clambered over Reed, saying, "It's Ramon. I re-organized the kitchen last night. I bet he's home for lunch and can't find anything to eat. He's probably having a heart attack. Gotta take this. Be right back."

Reed slid over into Doug's spot, pulling out his phone and clicking around as Jamie jabbered on about the kids. Grey was pretty tired of hearing about them, frankly, and was tempted to pull his phone out and ignore the conversation, too.

All of a sudden Reed laughed, and exclaimed, "I always knew

this guy was gay!" Then Reed flipped his phone around, showing a gossip site with a fuzzy picture of a celebrity on the landing page.

Jamie reached out to grab the phone from Reed's hands, and Caldwell said, "Oh, Reed, you don't want to read that—"

Reed held the phone out of Jamie's reach. "Why not? I mean, it's not like it's a secret." He looked back down at the screen. "The guy oozes gayness. I never believed that whole thing about—" Reed broke off, his eyes widening, and his lower lip going between his teeth. "Uncle Grey—"

Grey reached out and grabbed the phone from him.

Actor Scott Alpine, Gay!

The accompanying photograph left little to the imagination.

And just in case it wasn't clear who Scott Alpine was kissing, touching, maybe even fucking, though it was hard to tell by the angle and due to the fuzziness, the caption beneath it read: *Scott making love by the pool to his boyfriend of many years, out-and-proud Blaine Kellerman, CEO of Chill Blaine Enterprises.*

The first several lines of the article declared that the photographs had been obtained without James' knowledge by paparazzi who'd crept onto Mr. Kellerman's estate in Beverly Hills.

Grey quickly skimmed the article to see that Scott Alpine's people were stating adamantly that he and Mr. Kellerman were *just friends,* and that the photos misrepresented friendly affection between two old buddies.

"Grey—" Jamie started.

"Grey, I'm sorry," Caldwell said, solemnly.

"What for?" Grey asked, his voice unnaturally tight. "We aren't married. There are no locks on our doors." The words were automatic, rote, hollow.

Grey looked up to see Reed's face crumpling, sadness and

confusion warring there.

"Reed, it's okay."

Reed stood up, shaking his head and starting toward the exit.

Grey grabbed his wrist, saying, "Really, it's okay—"

But Reed jerked away and ran out the door. Grey looked back down at the phone in his hands, pocketed it carefully, and dropped a fifty-dollar bill on the table. Ignoring Jamie and Caldwell's objections about the money, he followed his nephew outside.

Reed stood on the corner, lighting a cigarette with a trembling hand.

Grey snatched it from his lips. "Since when do you smoke?"

"Since today."

Grey shook his head, and flipped the cigarette around, taking it for himself. "No, you don't. Don't let me catch you smoking again."

Reed sniffed, and turned his head away. "Why? What are you going to do? Ground me?"

Grey remained silent, rubbing his fingers over his eyes. How was he supposed to handle this situation?

"That's why you were mad at him yesterday, isn't it? That's why you wouldn't take his calls? He's been cheating on you? All this time?" Reed phrased everything as a question, his hurt obvious in the lift at the end of each sentence.

Grey flicked the cigarette, and decided on the truth. "Yes, that's why I wasn't taking his calls, but Reed—we aren't like your moms. We aren't married and we haven't made any promises of monogamy."

Not that he hadn't hoped for such promises for the first time in his stupid ass life.

Reed's voice trembled. "The article said that he's Scott Alpine's boyfriend, like he'd been his boyfriend for years."

Grey shook his head. "That's just the media trying to sell shit. Before Blaine and I got together, he was living with his business partner, Mark Vanderhalder, not Scott Alpine."

"You're not monogamous?" Reed asked coming back to that as Grey had known he would.

"Sometimes sex doesn't mean anything," Grey said. Except when it did mean something, and that was what had Grey's stomach in knots about Scott Alpine. "Do you understand? Sometimes it's just sex, Reed."

"How many other people are you fucking?"

Grey took a deep breath. He had to be careful what he said. If he played this the wrong way, then Reed would never forgive Blaine. It had to be on both of them. "As many as we want. Anyone we want."

"So you're a slut? A whore? Both of you?" Reed grew more agitated, his black hair swinging down into his eyes, and his cheeks flushing bright pink. "You fuck anything? Anything at all?"

Grey reached out to touch him, but Reed jerked away. "Reed, it's not like that. You're thinking the way you've been taught to think, along the traditional lines of love and marriage and someone with a baby carriage. We're gay men, Reed. That's not necessarily how it works for Blaine and me."

"That's how it is with Jamie and Caldwell." Then his face blanched. "Isn't it?"

"That's their business."

"Take me home," Reed said, shakily, turning his back on Grey. "I want to go home."

• • •

Fawn sat on the couch next to Grey stroking a hand through his hair soothingly. Grey had tossed his phone open to the gossip at her when she'd looked to him for answers as to why Reed had torn up the stairs to his bedroom and slammed the door.

She'd looked it over and then pulled Grey to sit on the couch, clucking and trying to mother him. He was letting her for the time being, but only because it was either that or scream at her to leave him the fuck alone, and Reed was already upset enough without adding that. He closed his eyes, annoyed that he was now someone who put another person first, missing the days of self-indulgence and acting on impulse.

"Grey, are you okay?" Fawn asked for the fifth time.

"Yes, goddammit, I'm fucking fine. It's Reed who's upset." Grey knew that wasn't entirely true, but until he had some time to himself, he wasn't sure that he could tease out the threads of his distress—what part was about Blaine? And what part was about the reaction that'd been set off in Reed?

"Yes, well…I know that he was hopeful you'd found someone special in Blaine. He really liked him, you know."

Grey ran a hand over his face. "Well, he can keep on liking him. He's still special. And if he's been with this Scott Alpine guy, then it's just—fucking." His chest felt empty when he said those words, but he needed to believe they were true.

"You've been apart for a long time. Ten years. A few months isn't going to make up for all the events that have happened in between, Grey. You've both changed, grown, become *men*. You have different priorities now. You might not be able to work those out between you."

Grey didn't want to hear any more. Fawn knew him too well, and it was like she'd tapped into his brain, streaming his thoughts out her mouth.

He stood up. "I have to go. Christ—" He looked up the stairs toward Reed's room, and sighed. "Tell him that—I love him. I've just got to go."

Then he headed upstairs to pack his things.

CHAPTER EIGHTEEN

GREY SIPPED A glass of Beam while he waited for the airline attendant to let him know that he could turn on his laptop. He'd left without stopping by the Nashville Blackburn Advertising offices to raise hell and chew new assholes, and he knew that word on the street would be that he was too distraught over Blaine to come by, but he didn't care. He wondered if he was going soft in old age.

His fingers curled around the glass again, and he swirled the liquid over his tongue, enjoying the burn as it went down. He could afford to drink more expensive bourbon, but the comfort of the tried and true appealed to him.

Grey shifted and pulled his phone out of his pocket, searching for any new photos or information on Blaine and Scott Alpine. A few new photos had surfaced. The first was clear enough to make out Blaine's laughing mouth and Scott Alpine's obviously wandering hands. The next picture was much more compromising, but for some reason it bothered him less than the one where Blaine was grinning that Doll Face smile that he was famous for.

He shoved the magazine back into his briefcase and looked out the window at the sun setting in the west. It was still light where Blaine was all the way across the continent.

Grey decided to call him when he got home.

The silence of his apartment was different from the silence of suburbia. It was punctuated by the sounds of the city rolling in.

Shouts, laughter, and the occasional siren, all broke the silence into manageable pieces, flowing like water over the hours, separating time. It was completely unlike the blanket of silence that had engulfed Grey at Jeanine and Fawn's house. He breathed in deeply, feeling himself relax and release Nashville to the past again.

He stood with his shoulder leaning against the doorjamb, looking out into the skyline, thinking of the time difference between New York and California—three hours. It was only nine o'clock where Blaine was. Way too early to even get started clubbing.

Their last conversation had been exactly what Grey hated most about 'relationships'. He'd acted the part of the broken-hearted fool in love, and Blaine had played out the role of the rogue who just didn't know any better.

Christ, it made his skin crawl to recognize such weakness in himself. Maybe this was what he'd protected himself against all of those years ago. Maybe part of him had suspected that he'd end up a sucker-punched lesbian, because he'd never managed to do anything halfway in his entire life.

And that pissed him off the most, because Grey Blackburn wasn't a failure. Grey Blackburn was a big, fat, fucking success and to feel like he was losing at something as important to him as Blaine infuriated him.

He stepped out into the night, leaning against the railing that separated him from certain death. Once he'd dreamed of having the world at his feet. Grey sighed and rested his elbows on the rail, staring down into the street, always flowing with passers-by, and wondered when he'd decided to settle for having Blaine at his feet.

The house phone caught his attention and he nearly stumbled

trying to get to it before the person hung up. The caller ID was a disappointment, though, and Grey nearly didn't answer.

"Grey, darling, I was just ringing to find out how you're holding up under the media deluge that Blaine's little escapade has set off."

Grey collapsed onto the sofa, cradling the phone to his ear and closing his eyes. "Dominique, what a surprise."

"My sources tell me that poor Scott Alpine is hopelessly out-ed."

Grey snorted. "What are your sources? NBC, CBS, Entertainment Tonight? It's every-fucking-where, Dominique."

"I told you Blaine liked drama, didn't I, darling? Now do you believe me?"

Grey grunted in response, not really sure of what he wanted to say in return to that.

"What does Blaine have to say for himself?" Dominique pushed on.

"Very little," Grey said, consulting his cell phone again. He had a few messages from Blaine, but he was afraid to read them.

"Well, what a tangled web my favorite little producer has woven for himself. Mark, you, and Scott Alpine all in a few months span. Even Blaine's head must be whirling from the debris of his personal tornado."

"As always, it's been a thrill, Dominique, but I've got to cut you loose."

"You used to be a much better source, Grey. Now you're all elusive and aloof. How will I ever convince you to sleep with me if I never see you anymore?"

Grey chuckled half-heartedly. "If you want to see me, Dominique, all you have to do is call Amelia to set an appointment. You know that."

"You don't want me! You just want my money!" Dominique exclaimed in faux irritation.

"Money turns me on like few things on earth," Grey said, recognizing the old banter that thankfully signaled the end of their conversation.

When the phone call finally ended, he closed his eyes and slid down on the sofa, clutching his cellphone to his chest.

· · ·

"GREY."

Grey squeezed his eyes shut, but a hand ran down his cheek gently, coaxing him from his dreams.

"Grey, wake up."

Blaine's voice reached around his consciousness and snatched him back to the here and now. Grey jerked awake, blinking up at Blaine's close-lipped smile.

"What the fuck are you doing here? And, fuck, what time is it?" He felt hung over, drugged, and he sat up groggily.

Blaine sat beside him on the sofa, his coat still on, and the scent of winter New York air still clinging to him.

"I flew in tonight. All hell broke loose out there, and besides, I needed to see you. You weren't taking my phone calls. And now Reed won't take my calls either. It's feeling all too familiar, Grey. I thought we had an agreement, a commitment to make it work this time? We weren't going just walk away when things got a little—uncomfortable."

"Wait, why the fuck are you calling Reed?"

Blaine blew out an exasperated puff of air. "Aren't you listening? You wouldn't answer your phone. I knew that you'd taken Reed home to Nashville, so I called Reed. The first time was okay, but when I called this afternoon—"

"He wouldn't talk to you?"

Blaine bit his lip, obviously fighting a strong emotion, finally saying, "Actually he did. And he said he never wanted to talk to me again. He said that he hates me, and that I—" Blaine broke off. "I guess he saw the news."

"You could say that. It's kind of hard to miss."

"Fuck," Blaine pressed his fingertips to his eyelids. "Christ. Fucking paparazzi."

Grey stood up, moving away from Blaine. "I'm tired. I can't talk about this now."

Blaine's eyes flashed dangerously, but then he lowered his head and acquiesced, saying, "I'm tired, too. It's late. Nearly two in the morning. There were delays at the airport."

"How'd you get in?" Grey suddenly asked, the doorman should have buzzed him.

Blaine blushed. "I bribed the guy downstairs."

"With a blowjob?"

"Ha! No, of course not." Blaine shook his head. "No, I gave him a signed copy of the L.A. Times with me and Scott Alpine on the front page. He said he'd sell it online for a shitload of money."

"I hope it's a pretty enough penny to cover his bills since he'll be out of a job."

Blaine sighed, standing up and peeling off his coat. "C'mon Grey. Let's go to bed."

"Aren't you being a little presumptuous?"

What was he doing? Grey *wanted* Blaine to stay the night, *wanted* to take his clothes off and fuck him for two weeks straight, but the fact that Blaine had manipulated his way into the penthouse, and now seemed ready to climb into Grey's bed for a good night's rest pissed him off.

"Um, am I?" Blaine asked, his fingers stilling on the buttons of his jeans.

Grey crossed his arms and glared. "I think you should go back to the hotel. Call me tomorrow. I'll answer the phone."

Blaine shifted uncomfortably. "I can't. Well, I *could*, but not really. I mean, I kind of checked out, and—"

Grey blinked, shaking his head in confusion. "What the fuck?"

"I told you I had business to take care of in New York this past weekend," Blaine said calmly, as though those words would clarify things.

"But you weren't *in* New York this past weekend."

Blaine sighed, running a hand over his hair, and scratching at his ear. "Yeah, fuck—but I meant to be. Sometimes I have really fucking bad ideas, and I guess this was one of them."

"You? Tell me something I don't know."

"I was going to surprise you by moving in while you were gone. You've mentioned it a few times now, and—"

"And so you just thought you'd move all of your things in here without asking me?" Grey knew he was queening out, but he went with it. "You were just going to surprise me by invading my home with your crap and your bullshit lies—"

"I never fucking lied to you!" Blaine spat out, instantly angry.

"'I have business in New York, Grey. I have business in L.A. that I have to take care of in person,'" Grey mocked.

"Well, I did."

"Yes, I guess it's rather hard to fuck someone when they're three thousand miles away."

"You think I fucked him?" Blaine stared at him, throat working. "Fuck you."

There was silence then. A long, hideous silence while Grey wrestled with the desire to strike where it would hurt, to say something to end everything once and for all, because he wasn't cut out for this shit.

Finally Blaine said icily, "I was going to surprise you by moving in while you were gone. When Mark called with the change in plans, I had my assistants check me out of the Plaza and box up my things. They're in storage. I'd planned to bring them here when I got back into town."

Grey glared at him.

Blaine went on, his voice slow and hard, "I heard from a friend that Scott was in L.A. so I called him from the airport. We hung out. He tried to start something, but nothing happened. He copped a feel. Big deal."

Grey waved his hand. "Right."

Blaine blinked, mouth settling into a thin line. "Fuck you, Grey. I bailed on the meetings with Sony when I realized that you were freaking out and that something was wrong with Reed. I'm here, aren't I? My priorities are loud and clear, right now. What are yours? Running away because things are hard?"

Grey ran a hand over his face and moved toward Blaine, surprised when Blaine didn't back away. He put his hand on the back of Blaine's neck, dipped his head to touch Blaine's forehead with his own, and whispered, "Blaine, I shouldn't have—"

"Yeah, you shouldn't have." Blaine stood stiffly, but didn't pull away.

Grey wrapped Blaine in his arms, hugging him tightly, forcing the stiffness out of him. "I was angry."

"You were jealous," Blaine said.

Grey was silent, burying his face in Blaine's neck, and breathing in.

Blaine went on, "I used to like to fuck him for fun. But I never loved him. I love *you*."

Grey shrugged, his heart thudding dully.

Blaine continued, "You and I, we've never discussed rules or monogamy. I didn't think we needed to this time around. I thought we both understood what we wanted."

They stood together quietly for a while, practicing synchronized breathing. Grey wanted to stop the conversation, wanted to suck red marks into the pale line of Blaine's neck, take off his clothes, push his knees up by his ears and fuck him. But—

"Things are different this time, you're right," Grey said, pulling away, and keeping his hand on the back of Blaine's neck. "I've changed and what I need in a—" Grey swallowed, rolled his eyes "—a relationship is different now. It's been ten years."

Grey chewed his lip and turned his back, looking out the window into the twinkling night, trying to understand what it was that he was feeling. Blaine's arms wrapped around him from behind, and he slid under Grey's arm, kissing the side of his neck. "What are you thinking, Grey?"

Grey shoved away, annoyed with himself, and with Blaine for putting him in this position, for making him feel these things, for being twelve years younger, and for not understanding.

Blaine sighed. "You can't even admit that you're jealous?"

"Fine, I'm fucking jealous. I acted like a fucking housewife. I know," Grey yelled. "But, that's not where it ends and begins anymore. I have Reed to worry about. And fuck, I never thought I'd hear myself say these words, but I want to live a life that he's proud of, and if my lover keeps ending up on the front page of every goddamn paper in America—"

"It wasn't supposed to happen—"

"Lots of shit isn't *supposed* to happen, Blaine. Babies aren't *supposed* to be born with AIDS, chocolate isn't *supposed* to be consumed as an alternative to anti-depressants, monkeys aren't *supposed* to be used for experi—"

"Okay, I fucking get it!"

"But, Reed has to come first for me, or at least really fucking high at the top of the list. He's counting on me to be his father figure. And I can't expect that he should come first for you, too. This—" Grey gestured between them "—is all too complicated. I was wrong to think it could work. I—"

"Grey, stop it," Blaine said, clamping his hand down on Grey's arm, pulling him close. "No. You can't fucking do this, because you promised me, and I told you—" Blaine's voice rose incrementally in a near panic. "I told you this time it was forever, and you agreed. That's a fucking commitment, goddamn it. That's a fucking *promise*, and this one little goddamn indiscretion isn't going to change a fucking thing, because *I don't care what you think*. You don't have the first clue—"

"I want to be monogamous."

"Me too."

Grey stared at him, shocked that Blaine's words hit him so hard that he felt sick.

In a good way.

"I'm in love with you. I always have been. And I want to only be with you." Blaine laughed. "I thought you understood."

Grey kissed him, silencing his words by sucking his tongue into his mouth.

Teeth and nails said as much as words for a change. Blaine bit Grey's bicep, scratched down his back, and writhed beneath him. It was easy enough to move from wrestling to fucking.

Grey thrust solidly, throwing his head back, and pounding Blaine into the floor. Blaine's back made slapping, sliding sounds along the wood as they rutted together, desperate and needy.

"Oh, God, oh fuck," Blaine moaned, his toes curling by Grey's ears and his back arching up like a bow. Grey kissed his lips, as Blaine shot load after load onto their chests and stomachs. "Oh, God, Grey—"

Grey grabbed Blaine's wrists, pulled them over his head, and rammed into Blaine hard. He came, crying out, and afterwards they kissed tenderly, shuddering through their aftershocks.

Sweaty, curled together on the floor, Blaine whispered, "Christ, you are such a drama queen."

Grey whapped him on the chest with the back of one hand and snorted.

CHAPTER NINETEEN

THE NEXT MORNING they ate at the diner around the corner and read the gossip sites on their phone.

"Anonymous fucks," Grey stated, sipping his coffee. "Scott Alpine's been engaging in Grindr anonymous fucks."

"Sounds about right," Blaine took a bite out of a biscuit and chewed thoughtfully.

Grey went on, "How he thought he'd keep that quiet, I don't know."

Blaine nodded. "I don't think that Scott's going to be that disheartened by all these revelations. I don't think he's actually trying to rebuild his image as a heterosexual. Pretty sure he's fucking relieved to be out."

"And I can't believe we managed to dodge those reporters this morning. Christ, are you going to make a statement or what?"

Blaine sighed, running a hand over his hair. "I'm thinking that it wouldn't be entirely untruthful to say that Scott Alpine and I are just friends. I mean, that's all we are...just friends. Who've fucked in the past. No one needs to know that part, though. What do you think?"

"I think it's not lying when—"

"When they camp outside the door of your boyfriend's apartment building screaming for a statement?"

Grey chuckled. "Yeah. Who spilled the beans on that anyway? Scott—trying to cover his ass?"

"A little too late for that since his ass will be on the cover of People this week," Blaine said. "Yeah, it could've been Scott. Or Mark. Like I said, he still hasn't found a new place to live in L.A. and he's not feeling especially generous with me right now."

Grey smiled grimly. "What the fuck did you expect, Doll Face? A fucking Best Wishes card and some flowers? Are you really that obtuse?"

"No. I just don't like knowing I fucked him over. That's why I didn't make a big deal about how long he was taking to get out of the house." Blaine sighed. "I care about him."

"I know."

"Anyway, I think he's getting out now, though. When he went off on me about Scott being there, I may have said something about a restraining order and he got kind of upset." Blaine was blushing, obviously embarrassed by his antics. "Christ, maybe *I'm* the drama queen."

"You said it."

Blaine winced. "I handled everything with Mark so badly. I'm going to miss him as a partner and a friend."

"He's leaving Chill Blaine?"

"No, but he's taking some distance. We won't be working together much for a long time."

Grey felt sorry for the bastard. Loving Blaine wasn't easy. And it was hell when Blaine didn't love you back. "You were a dick to him."

"I know, but, still, fuck you."

Grey checked his watch. "Okay, but I have to be at work in an hour for an appointment with Bosendorfer pianos, so if you could just crawl under the table and suck me off, that'd be a lot more efficient."

Blaine kicked him, grinning cheekily, and Grey felt most of

the heaviness that had been weighing him down lift off, carried away in a balloon of hope.

"Besides, I learned from the best," Blaine said, half-laughing.

"How to give blow jobs? Why yes, you did."

"I meant how to be a drama queen. And an asshole."

Grey kicked him under the table hard, and smiled when Blaine yelped. "So are you going to move in with me or what?"

"You know the trick to living together, don't you?"

Grey lifted a brow.

"It's like fucking. Sometimes it's hard and fast, sometimes it's sweet and slow, and sometimes you're tired, and it's boring and annoying, but you keep on doing it, and—"

"You come screaming my name in the end."

Blaine nodded. "Every fucking time."

* * *

REED WAS ANOTHER matter.

Grey didn't think it should be harder to make up with his nephew than it had been to make up with Blaine.

"Fawn, he won't even talk to me," Grey said, leaning back in his office chair and kicking his feet on the desk. "I mean, so I used to fuck a lot of people? What's the big deal?"

He knew what the big deal was; he just didn't want to admit it. He'd been hoping that Fawn would convince Reed to brush it under the carpet, too.

"He's already different, Grey. He's already got so much to deal with being a boy with two moms and no real dad, especially with no straight man around at all. Except for Mama's Roy. Who he's never really liked that much because he says he smells funny."

"He does smell funny," Grey asserted.

Fawn ignored him. "So, right now, when Reed's confused, and tired of being different, when he's worried that he's maybe gay, or maybe straight, or bi, or pan, or who knows, and when he's starting to hope that there isn't that big of a difference between them all, maybe he can be gay and still have a 'normal' life—"

"There's no such thing as a 'normal' life, Fawn."

"Grey, don't you remember being fourteen and wanting to be normal? Don't you remember how horrifying it was to start to see the ways in which your parents and the people you admired weren't perfect?"

"I always knew our parents weren't fucking perfect. I was never allowed that little delusion."

"Reed isn't you."

"Thank fucking God for that."

"You said it," Fawn murmured.

Grey remained silent for a moment, tired of the persona that he had to adopt just to make it through these conversations. He was so tired of pretending things didn't hurt him that hurt other people. He didn't even know why he did it. Fawn could see right through him anyway.

"So, how do I fix it?"

"Give him some time. He'll come around."

Grey sighed. "And what about his Christmas break?"

"I'll have to get back to you."

● ● ●

"BLUE," GREY SAID, not looking up from his phone. He'd taken it with him into the dressing room where Blaine had piled up loads of winter clothes to try on. Now he was currently fielding some emails and darting glances up at Blaine's choices.

"I like red," Blaine replied, and out of the corner of his eye, Grey could see him holding up a red sweater.

"Blue."

Blaine pawed through a few more items. "Maybe black?"

"Blue."

Later, with Blaine fitting perfectly under his arm, they walked toward the apartment they now shared. He admired the way Blaine's hair flickered gold and blond in the near-winter sunlight. The blue winter coat brought out Blaine's eyes, and when he glanced up at Grey, smiling and still talking about the initial drawings he'd been reviewing for *A Soviet Mole*, Grey thought his heart had literally missed a beat.

His joy was snuffed a little later that night when Grey sat at the dining room table, the phone cradled to his ear as he listened to Reed make a lame excuse about Christmas break.

"I've just got too much make-up work to do from that week I came up before. Maybe I can see you at Spring Break. Or next summer."

Blaine was pretending not to listen, head down and supposedly absorbed in working out the storyboard for *A Soviet Mole*, but Grey knew Blaine was worried too and taking in every word.

"You could work on that stuff here. Blaine and I would be glad to help you." Grey hated that he sounded desperate. He hated even more that Reed knew that Grey knew Reed was lying.

"Thanks, Grey, but I think I'd better just stay home."

Grey chewed on his bottom lip, ran his finger along the edge of the table, and tried to think of something to say that would bring back the kid who'd begged to live with him, who'd taken a bus up the eastern seaboard to see him.

He took a deep breath and said, "Reed, you haven't called me 'Uncle Grey' since I last saw you. You won't take my phone calls. You won't come see me. It's not the fucking homework. It's what we talked about before I left town. You're angry with me."

Reed was silent.

"You're angry with me because I said that Blaine and I used to sleep with a lot of other men."

"You're not only gay, but you're a fucking whore," Reed hissed.

Grey cleared his throat, surprised at the pain he felt hearing those words. "Reed, I—"

A dial tone sang in his ear. He lowered his head into his hands and swallowed around the tightness in his throat. He didn't know if he was glad or not, because while he and Blaine were monogamous now, there was nothing wrong with fucking a lot men. There was nothing wrong with that at all.

Soon Blaine was massaging his neck and shoulders, saying softly, "It's okay, Grey. He'll come around."

Grey wasn't so sure about that.

•   •   •

"HEY JAMIE. WHAT'S up?" Grey stood on the terrace smoking a cigarette, staring off into the distance. Blaine was asleep in the bed, but Grey hadn't been tired and so he'd given into the temptation of a smoke.

"You, apparently. Christ, it's after midnight. Something better be wrong, or I'm gonna be really pissed."

Grey said nothing. His throat hurt, and he blinked against the stupid wetness that came to his eyes.

"Shit," Jamie sighed. "Fuck, hold on. I'm getting out of bed."

Grey heard him say to Caldwell, "Something's really wrong with Grey. No, no—it's okay. Not deathly wrong or anything. Go back to sleep."

Grey flicked his cigarette ash, and asked, "How can I be so happy and so fucking miserable? This fucking sucks."

"Is it Blaine? I thought you two had worked it—"

"No." Grey sighed, cleared his throat and repeated, "No. It's Reed."

Jamie let out a relieved sound, almost chuckling. "What'd he say? That he hated you? Hoped you'd die?"

"Mm, nothing that drastic, but close enough."

"They all say that. Didn't you say that to our folks?"

"I meant it…at least when it came to Pa."

"Right. Well…I hear it from our fosters all the time, and they don't fucking mean it."

"Reed means it." He blew out a stream of smoke.

"How long can he be angry with you, Grey? Give it some time. He'll come around."

"I'm so fucking sick of people saying that." Grey dragged on his cigarette.

"He will!" Jamie exclaimed. "Just be patient."

"I don't think so, Jamie."

"Listen, take my word on it," Jamie sounded dismissive. "I've been there. I know first hand what raising a teenager is like. Remember? Our third foster, Samson, used to say all kinds of shit."

"It's different."

"How so?"

"Because I've been a crap dad. I promised Fawn I'd be a great dad to her kid, and I wasn't. I was utter shit."

He was relieved when Jamie didn't deny it.

The sounds from the street floated up to Grey, and he looked down to watch a man and woman trudge by with a couple of dogs. He took deep breaths, listening to Jamie's steady breathing at the other end of the line.

"Hey, Jamie?"

"Yeah?"

"I love you."

Jamie let out a long sigh. "I love you too. And it's going to be okay, Grey. Kids do this. I promise."

When he crawled into bed, Blaine's body was warm next to him, and he curled in toward the heat, nuzzling Blaine's neck and cheek, feeling the drag of stubble over his lips.

"You're cold," Blaine murmured, rolling towards him and shuddering when Grey pressed his feet against Blaine's warm calves. "Were you outside?"

Grey made a noise of assent, slowly rolling his hips against Blaine's side. He slid his hand down and rubbed gentle circles around Blaine's belly button. "Warm me up."

"You smell like cigarettes."

"That a problem?"

"Not really." Blaine pushed up to kiss Grey's lips, cupping his face with one hand, and grasping his hair with the other. "Fuck me," he whispered against Grey's lips.

Grey moved down the bed, lifted Blaine's legs under the knees, and pushed them high, exposing Blaine's ass. Grey sucked hard kisses on Blaine's inner thighs, holding him down when Blaine thrashed, half-laughing, and half-moaning with the good kind of pain.

His tongue moved toward Blaine's hole, lapping hot paths of wetness over the pale skin and the red marks he'd just made. Blaine went very still, no longer writhing, holding his breath in anticipation. Grey dragged his tongue slowly, and when he licked over Blaine's asshole, he gripped Blaine's thighs hard to hold him down.

"Fuck!" Blaine tensed all over, his body already shaking with want.

Grey kissed his ass cheeks then moved in to tongue-fuck his hole, driving in as deeply as possible. Blaine bucked, his asshole opening under Grey's tongue.

"Oh, fuck me, fuck me—"

Grey grabbed a condom and lube, working some slickness into Blaine.

"Hold on," Grey said, rolling the condom on. "Just a second."

Blaine reached for him, grabbed his hair, and pulled him up, kissing him hard. Grey tried to pull back, but Blaine had too tight a grip on his hair, so Grey lined up to the best of his ability, and pushed against the first ring of muscle.

Blaine moaned into Grey's mouth, intensifying the kiss, and Grey ran his hands soothingly down Blaine's sides as he slid in.

"Ahhh," Blaine whimpered, and Grey held still for just a moment, adjusting his position.

"Better?" he asked.

Blaine answered by grabbing his ass and pulling him flush.

As Grey slid all the way in, Blaine arched up to meet him, wrapping his legs around Grey's waist, kicking Grey's ass with his heels.

Grey began thrusting hard, watching the play of expressions over Blaine's face: the open mouthed astonishment, the glazed look of bliss, and the hot, fierce look of love.

Grey drove into him, reaching between them to help Blaine with stroking his cock. He sped up his motion as he watched

Blaine draw closer to orgasm, the red flush creeping up Blaine's chest and igniting his cheeks.

Blaine's eyes squeezed shut, and his fingers gripped Grey's arms, nails digging in to leave marks.

The low, stuttering noises that sometimes came before orgasm poured out of Blaine as he writhed. Grey jerked Blaine's cock harder, and then slammed into him when he cried out. Blaine shuddered and jerked as his come spurted between them.

Grey was so close, close enough to taste it, but he slowed down, watching Blaine's eyes blink in confusion. "Blaine—"

Blaine reached out to touch his cheek, staring up at him open and giving.

Grey stopped thrusting altogether, gazing at Blaine's face, memorizing his red lips, his shining blue eyes.

"Blaine—"

Blaine put a finger on his lips, halting his words. "Shh."

Grey took a deep breath, kissed Blaine's finger, and moved it away from his mouth. "I love you."

Blaine's eyes closed for a moment then opened them again, whispering fiercely, "Prove it."

Grey gripped Blaine's chin, kissed his mouth with a hunger that he didn't think he'd ever be able to satisfy, driving into him as hard and fast as he possibly could. He felt Blaine's body give beneath him, heard the harsh exhalations as Grey pummeled him, giving him everything that he had, pouring himself into it.

And as he shook and quivered through his orgasm, he heard Blaine whisper, "I believe you."

CHAPTER TWENTY

GREY TRIED TO call Reed again several days later, then once again a week after that. But there was never any answer, and Fawn said to just leave it alone for a while. But it ate at him that his nephew wouldn't speak to him—that Reed wouldn't even let him try to explain.

In the office, Amelia was all smiles and rainbows because she and the beautiful librarian were getting married. Grey kept his eyes focused on his work, as Blaine, who was visiting him for lunch break, feigned interest in her wedding plans.

Amelia had just described the ideas they had for wedding vows, and Blaine had murmured with appropriately attentive noises, when she concluded with, "Now, we just need to get someone to plan the event because neither one of us has the time to do it right."

Grey, flipping through contracts for some new accounts, said casually, "What the fuck is this? Why isn't this page signed?"

Amelia came around his desk and grabbed the contract from him, her excitement replaced with an all-business demeanor. "Oh, my mistake. I'll rectify it immediately, Mr. Blackburn."

"Do that. If you can't get it fixed by midnight, then you're fired."

Amelia stuck out her tongue, and Grey smiled. She was finally getting the hang of working with him.

"God, that was hot," Blaine said when Amelia shut the door

on her way out. "Let's call her back in here, and you can fire her for real, then I'll fuck you on the sofa."

Grey chuckled. "Go work on something for another thirty. I need to finish this before we can go. Don't you have a fucking company to run?"

Blaine sat down in one of the office chairs that Amelia used for filing. It spun back and forth, giving her the ability to work between two drawers. Blaine began twirling around in it, lifting his feet to get better spin.

"Mark's got it under control."

Grey's eyebrow went up and he leaned back in his chair. "Still trust him that much, do you?"

Blaine stopped spinning and nodded. "Yeah, I talked to him yesterday and he's dating someone new now, so—" Blaine shrugged and swallowed hard. "I'm glad for him. He sounded really happy."

"Jealous?"

Blaine scoffed. "Please, as if there is anything to be jealous about. I'm truly happy for him. He's such a good man and he deserves a lover who is as devoted to him as he used to be to me."

"Go Mark," Grey intoned dryly.

"Yeah," Blaine agreed. "You know, though. I'm thinking of retiring as CEO. I'd still own part of it, and I could count on Mark as a great replacement for me. He's part owner already, and with just a few more shares of stock in his name, then he'd be majority share owner."

Grey frowned. "I thought that Chill Blaine Enterprises was your baby, or some shit like that?"

Blaine shrugged. "It doesn't do it for me anymore. I think it was a fixation born out of romantic frustration."

The idea of Blaine giving up his business was unsettling, and

Grey flipped through another stack of contracts before saying, "Maybe you should try a sabbatical before you give it up completely. Go to Italy. See some Old Masters, kiss the feet of the David, whatever—"

"You go with me."

"No can do, Doll Face. Not everyone has a Mark to run their lives for them." Grey didn't look up from his papers.

"Wouldn't you miss me?"

"Madly. Night and day." Grey made it sound sarcastic, but they both knew it was true.

"So, come. You know Phil down in Nashville would love the opportunity to try out his mojo as a New York big-wig."

"Are you insane?"

"Come with me." Blaine's voice grew excited. "I know! We could take Reed. For the summer."

Grey looked up in amusement. "Are you suggesting that I buy my nephew's affection back with a trip to Italy?"

"Yes!"

Grey grew very serious. "It…could work."

Blaine sighed, stood up, and stretched, his sweater lifting up to show his stomach. "Think it over. Seriously. It could be just the thing."

• • •

"I'VE BEEN TO Italy," Reed said the next day. "Summer house, hello? Duh."

Fawn had pretty much forced him to take Grey's call, but Grey didn't plan to waste it. "I know, kiddo, but this would be different."

"Why?"

"Well," Grey tried to think of something fucking amazing that would make this the best trip in the entire world for a fourteen year old. "Because it will be me, you, and Blaine—as a family."

God, that sounded fucking lame even to him, *especially* to him.

"And what about Blaine's *boyfriend*? Is he gonna come, too?"

Grey sighed. "Reed, that's in the past. Blaine and I really want you on this trip. We want to be a part of your life."

"What if I don't want to be part of yours?"

Grey shook his head. He couldn't understand how the things that Reed said to him could cut him to the quick. He'd thought he had tougher skin than that.

The dial tone wasn't a surprise.

Fawn called about ten minutes after Reed had hung up the phone. "He'll spend this summer in Italy with you, Grey. I'll see to it."

It wasn't what he wanted to hear, but he supposed it was better than nothing.

Blaine began making lists of things they'd need on their trip and then handed the work off to his very competent assistants. And Grey actually flew Phil up to meet with the representatives from Nike, Tiffany's, and Captain Bacon. If he handled the meetings to Grey's satisfaction, then he'd set Phil up at the Plaza to handle things while they were in Italy.

He called Jamie from the terrace in the middle of a snowstorm to tell him that he was drunk as hell and missed him, and that Blaine couldn't be Supergirl to his Superman, because that's what little brothers were for, right?

Jamie agreed, saying that Superman was fucking Lex Luthor, or Batman, or both anyway—then they'd spent an hour trying to decide which one Blaine was, and then hypothesizing huge superhero orgies with extra-strong condoms to contain the superhero spooge.

When Grey was frozen to the bone, he hung up the phone, and went back into the penthouse. He fucked Blaine over the dining room table, and then again in the warm shower, because he was still cold as hell.

Two days before he was supposed to pick Reed up at the airport, Fawn called frantic. Reed was missing. He'd left a note saying that he was going away for a while and not to worry. He'd also turned off his phone's tracking app and wasn't picking up or responding texts.

Jeanine was having contractions, Fawn was having hysterics, and Grey didn't know what to do, so he called Mama.

"Don't fucking flip out, you hear me?" Mama shouted into the phone. "Reed's a smart boy with a good head on his shoulders. Plus he's got his phone. He'll be all right."

But Grey could hear the doubt in her voice. "Don't lie to me. He's out there somewhere, Mama, and I'm going to come back to Nashville to find him."

He packed an overnight bag while Blaine paced anxiously. "What should I do? How can I help?"

"Just stay here and answer phone calls. Maybe he'll call the landline."

Grey tried to forget that Reed hadn't called him in months. He grabbed items of clothing, and stuffed them in the bag, his heart trip-hammering in his chest.

CHAPTER TWENTY-ONE

NASHVILLE WAS ALWAYS the same. Grey stalked the familiar streets, fear building in his gut. Jeanine was in the hospital, probably giving birth to the new baby right that moment. Mama and Jamie were all there to support her, while Fawn and Caldwell tried to convince the police to waive the twenty-four hour requirement before they'd start looking for Reed.

Everyone and their brother had been contacted, and no one knew where Reed had gone. The only missing link was Jamie's oldest former foster kid, Samson, who had gone away for the Christmas break with his new girlfriend from law school.

So, Grey decided to start at Samson's place. Maybe Reed had a key…or maybe he'd just broken in.

The address was in a not-so-great part of town, and when he looked through the windows and saw a dark head of hair watching television, he didn't know if he'd ever been so relieved, so happy, or so fucking pissed off in his entire life.

He knocked on the door, calling out, "Special delivery for the run-away."

A long time passed, and Grey heard a door shut on the other side of the apartment. The little shit was trying to escape. He ran around back in time to see Reed scaling down the fire escape, and Grey started up after him. When he could, he grabbed Reed's legs and forced him down, holding him on the stairs.

"*Don't* you try to run away from me, kiddo. I came *all the way* from New York to find your ass, so *don't* you fucking run from me."

Reed's eyes were large, dark, and afraid. He shook a little in Grey's grip, and didn't say anything.

Grey grabbed his arm, and dragged him down the fire escape ladder, holding on to him a little too roughly as he dug his cell phone out of a pocket.

"Fawn, I found him. I've got him right here. No, he's okay. He's fine." Grey thrust the phone to Reed's ear, saying, "Tell your mother that you're fucking fine."

Reed stammered, "I'm fine, Mom."

Grey took the phone back. "Now take a goddamn chill pill and get to your wife. I'll bring him home when I'm through with him."

Reed tried to jerk away, but Grey still had a height advantage and the strength of a grown man. He tumbled Reed to the ground, wrestling with him there, until he gained the upper hand.

"I said don't run from me, Reed. I fucking mean it."

Reed nodded, panting on the ground, and Grey finally let him up. They stood and stared at each other, dark hazel eyes grinding into a lighter pair.

"Do you really hate me that much that you'd run away from home, scare your mothers to death, just to avoid spending a holiday with me? And for what? Because I've fucked a lot of guys in my time? Because Blaine's fucked a lot of guys? I don't understand, Reed." Grey raked a hand through his hair. "Why are you so fucking angry?"

Reed's mouth began to tremble and he ducked his head.

"What? What is it?"

Reed sank to the ground and buried his head in his knees, his shoulders shaking with tears. Grey sat down beside him, resting his hand on Reed's back and waiting. The ground was cold and it seeped into his bones, making him shiver.

Finally Reed looked up, wiping tears and snot from his face with the back of a sleeve. "Um, so I fucked this guy at school—" Reed said in a whisper.

Grey lowered his head and closed his eyes.

"I used a condom, like you said," Reed went on, his breathing erratic. "It was in the locker rooms. After soccer practice."

"When was this?" Grey asked softly, opening his eyes and staring at the bleak Nashville apartment building in front of them.

"Last week."

Grey nodded, the ground chilling him completely. "And?"

"I'm sorry, Uncle Grey. I'm so, so, so sorry."

"That you fucked a guy at school? Or that you've been avoiding me?"

Reed sniffled and half-laughed. "I was so mad at you—I don't want to be queer, but I am. And when you said that, about fucking so many people, I didn't want that to be my life. Because everything has always been so fucked up for me, and I just got so fucking *pissed*."

Grey touched Reed's hair, ran his finger down Reed's cheek, and turned his chin so that he could look him in the eye. "I love you whether you're gay or straight or undecided. I love you whether you're a slut or a monogamous killjoy or an asexual virgin. I love you whether you call me a faggot, or a whore, or a slut. Anything you say to me, Reed, I can handle, and it won't change how I feel about you."

Reed, all five feet, ten inches of him, nearly crawled into Grey's lap, his arms tight around Grey's neck, and his breathing came fast and heavy as he fought off more tears.

"So this guy…is he your boyfriend?"

Reed hiccupped another sob and said, "I think so? Yeah. I guess. His name's Marco."

"Well, that's great, kiddo. That's wonderful."

• • •

THE NEW BABY was a boy, Abraham Jamie Rollins, and Reed seemed in awe of him. Grey hung back at the edge of the family, watching his pseudo-son hold his new little brother.

Jamie was nearly out of his mind with glee, telling everyone who would listen about the rigors of the birth, and how he'd held Jeanine's hand for the worst of it, and now had a baby named after him as a reward. Grey spent the rest of the afternoon warding off Jamie's ecstatic kisses and hugs.

When Blaine arrived on the scene, having caught the first plane available, Grey wrapped his arms around Blaine's neck, and leaned down to whisper, "I need to fuck you. I need to fuck you so hard."

Blaine smiled, kissed his lips, and said, "God, you're always such a romantic. Next thing you know, you'll be telling me how you're going to rim me for hours and then fist my ass until I pass out."

Grey lifted his brows provocatively, but then Blaine was smothered in Mama's kisses, Fawn's hugs, and he didn't escape Jamie's embrace, either.

Reed wandered up shyly, hugging Blaine with a tentative expression.

"Hey, kiddo. I'm really sorry for upsetting you," Blaine said. "I *never* want to upset you."

Reed ducked his head, mumbling. "S'okay. I'm a big dork, I guess."

"Nah, you're just a drama queen like your Uncle Grey. You come by it naturally, don't worry." Blaine grinned at Reed. "Although, you know, I did run away myself one time. I stole a—"

"Don't give him ideas," Grey said. "He's got plenty of his own."

Reed blushed, and Grey suspected he might have a crush on Blaine. Grey studied Blaine's smile, and shining blue eyes as he talked to Jeanine, Fawn, and Mama about his life. Blaine was radiant.

Then a young man came into the room with a small bouquet of flowers and Reed's ears turned the color of the roses. The dark haired, rosy-cheeked guy, introduced himself as Marco, and Reed brought him over to meet the baby Abraham.

Marco cooed and put his arm around Reed's shoulders, and then gave the most brilliant, charming smile as he was introduced to Fawn and Jeanine. Then, when it was time to meet Blaine and Grey, he was put out his hands and called them both sir. It was ridiculous and totally fucking adorable.

When Marco kissed Reed's cheek and congratulated him on being a big brother, Grey couldn't fault Reed for his taste.

CHAPTER TWENTY-TWO

THE PARTY WAS in full-tilt when Grey and Blaine arrived. Dominique greeted them at the door with kisses on both cheeks, and already seeking gossip.

"So, Blaine, my sources say that you're making arrangements to sell enough shares to Mark to make him majority shareholder in Chill Blaine Enterprises."

Blaine smirked. "Is your source Mark by any chance?"

"Now, darling, you know I never reveal such things, but yes."

Blaine chuckled. "Well, your source is right. Mark has a good grip on the company and I'm ready to move on."

Dominique turned to Grey. "And how was your trip to Italy? Was your beautiful boy the toast of the town everywhere he went?"

"Which one?" Grey joked, pulling Blaine close to his side.

"Good answer!" Dominique exclaimed. "I meant your nephew, but perhaps he's still too young to—" She became distracted, her gaze landing on a new arrival. "Oh, that's Miles Monroe. He actually bats for my team and I'm determined to have him. I'll be back. I'm not done with you, yet."

Grey ran his eyes over the party, seeing plenty of people that he might have chosen to fuck in the past. Instead, he turned to Blaine and whispered, "What do you say we hit the bathroom?"

Blaine seemed to have trouble containing his grin. "Christ, we just got here."

"There's no time like the present."

Five minutes later, Grey had Blaine's dress shirt shoved up, and Blaine's pants down around his ankles. He buried his nose in the back of Blaine's neck, breathing in his shampoo and soap scent, fucking him over Dominique's bathroom sink, while the party whirled on outside.

*   *   *

IT HAD BEEN in Rome, standing outside the Pantheon, when Reed had asked Grey to tell him about the first time he met Blaine.

Blaine and Reed sat on a bench ten yards away and he crossed to them to hear Blaine's answer. "He picked me up at a club and took me home. Relieved me of my virginity. It was a pretty intense start to our relationship."

"He was just a kid. And I thought he was fucking beautiful," Grey said, slipping in beside Reed.

"Was it like in the movies? Did you see him and boom! Love!"

Grey laughed. "No. Hardly."

But then he recalled the night he'd met Blaine, the moment he'd first seen him, and the sudden rush he'd felt, as though the entire world, no *universe*, had suddenly focused in on him and the dancing blond boy.

Grey thought that if he'd felt anything that night, he'd tried to bury it, and like all shallow graves, it had eventually given up its secret. Yes, he'd known. He just hadn't wanted to know.

"What about Marco?" Grey asked. He knew Reed had been texting the boy every day. "Was it like in the movies?"

"Maybe. He's pretty great." Reed's cheeks flushed. "I really like him."

Grey smirked, as Reed asked Blaine, "So what'd you think the first time you saw Uncle Grey?"

Blaine didn't look up from his phone, still poking away making notes about a new film idea that had come to him. He said, distractedly, "I thought he was everything I wanted. Why?"

"Just wondering," Reed answered. "Was he?"

Blaine grinned, looking up to catch Grey's eye. "Close enough."

Yes, what they had was everything. It was hard and easy, sweet and bitter, domestic and fun. It didn't matter what came, they'd whether it together. So long as he was with Blaine, Grey was ready for the future.

"And how do you feel about Blaine now?" Reed asked.

Grey took hold of Blaine's chin, gazed into his eyes, and said, "Bring on forever."

The End

Letter from Leta

Dear Reader,

Thank you so much for reading *Bring On Forever*! It's one of the first stories I ever wrote and I hope it felt special to you, too.

Be sure to follow me on BookBub or Goodreads to be notified of new releases. And look for me on Facebook for snippets of the day-to-day writing life, or join my Facebook Group for announcements and special giveaways. To see some sources of my inspiration, you can follow my Pinterest boards or Instagram.

If you enjoyed the book, please take a moment to leave a review! Reviews not only help readers determine if a book is for them, but also help a book show up in site searches.

Also, for the audiobook connoisseurs out there, many of my other books are available in that format. I hope to eventually add my entire backlist, including *Bring On Forever*, to my audiobook roster over the next few years.

Thank you for being a reader!

Leta

Book 1 in the Home for the Holidays series

MR. FROSTY PANTS

by Leta Blake

Frosty former friends get a steamy second chance in this Christmas gay romance!

Can true love warm his frozen heart?

When Casey Stevens went away to college four years ago, he ghosted on his straight best friend, Joel Vreeland. He hoped time and distance would lessen the unrequited affection he felt, but all it did was make him miss Joel more.

Home for the holidays, Casey hopes they might find a way to be friends again. But Joel's frosty reception reminds Casey of just how hard he had to fight to be Joel's friend in the first place. It's going to take a Christmas miracle to get past that cool façade again.

Joel isn't as straight as Casey believes, and his years of pining for Casey have left him hurting and alone, caring for his abusive father and struggling to get by. Unable to trust anyone except his rescue dog—and with no reason to believe Casey is interested in him for more than a holiday fling—Joel's icy heart might shatter before it can thaw.

Can Casey and Joel's love overcome mistrust, parental rejection, class differences, and four long years apart? *Mr. Frosty Pants* is a stand-alone, Christmas gay romance by Leta Blake featuring a virgin hero, childhood friends-to-lovers, second chance romance, and steamy mm first times.

ANY GIVEN LIFETIME
by Leta Blake

He'll love him in any lifetime.

Neil isn't a ghost, but he feels like one. Reincarnated with all his memories from his prior life, he spent twenty years trapped in a child's body, wanting nothing more than to grow up and reclaim the love of his life.

As an adult, Neil finds there's more than lost time separating them. Joshua has built a beautiful life since Neil's death, and how exactly is Neil supposed to introduce himself? As Joshua's long-dead lover in a new body? Heartbroken and hopeless, Neil takes refuge in his work, developing microscopic robots called nanites that can produce medical miracles.

When Joshua meets a young scientist working on a medical project, his soul senses something his rational mind can't believe. Has Neil truly come back to him after twenty years? And if the impossible is real, can they be together at long last?

Any Given Lifetime is a stand-alone, slow burn, second chance gay romance by Leta Blake featuring reincarnation and true love. This story includes some angst, some steam, an age gap, and, of course, a happy ending.

THE RIVER LEITH
by Leta Blake

Amnesia stole his memories, but it can't erase their love.

Leith is terrified after waking up in a hospital bed to find his most recent memories are three years out of date.

Worse, he can't even remember how he met the beautiful man who visits him most days. Everyone claims Zach is his best friend, but Leith's feelings for Zach aren't friendly.

They're so much more than that.

Zach fills Leith with longing. Attraction. Affection. **Lust.** And those feelings are even scarier than losing his memory, because Leith's always been straight. Hasn't he?

For Zach, being forgotten by his lover is excruciating. Leith's amnesia has stolen everything: their relationship, their happiness, and the man he loves. Suddenly single and alone, Zach knows nothing will ever be okay again.

Desperate to feel better, Zach confesses his grief to the faceless Internet. But his honesty might come back to haunt them both.

The River Leith is a standalone MM romance with amnesia trope, hurt/comfort, bisexual discovery, "first time" gay scenes, a second chance at first love, and a satisfying happy ending.

A lustful young alpha meets his match in an older omega with a past.

Professor Vale Aman has crafted a good life for himself. An unbonded omega in his mid-thirties, he's long since given up hope that he'll meet a compatible alpha, let alone his destined mate. He's fulfilled by his career, his poetry, his cat, and his friends.

When Jason Sabel, a much younger alpha, imprints on Vale in a shocking and public way, longings are ignited that can't be ignored. Fighting their strong sexual urges, Jason and Vale must agree to contract with each other before they can consummate their passion.

But for Vale, being with Jason means giving up his independence and placing his future in the hands of an untested alpha—as well as facing the scars of his own tumultuous past. He isn't sure it's worth it. But Jason isn't giving up his destined mate without a fight.

This is a gay romance novel, 118,000 words, with a strong happy ending, as well as a well-crafted, **non-shifter** omegaverse, with alphas, betas, omegas, male pregnancy, heat, and **knotting**. Content warning for pregnancy loss and aftermath.

Gay Romance Newsletter

Leta's newsletter will keep you up to date on her latest releases and news from the world of M/M romance. Join the mailing list today and you're automatically entered into future giveaways. letablake.com

Leta Blake on Patreon

Become part of Leta Blake's Patreon community in order to access exclusive content, deleted scenes, extras, bonus stories, rewards, prizes, interviews, and more. www.patreon.com/letablake

Other Books by Leta Blake

Any Given Lifetime
Mr. Frosty Pants
The River Leith
Smoky Mountain Dreams
Angel Undone
The Difference Between
Heat for Sale
Stay Lucky
Stay Sexy
Omega Mine: Search for a Soulmate
Bring on Forever
Raise Up Heart

The Home for the Holidays Series
Mr. Frosty Pants
Mr. Naughty List

The Training Season Series
Training Season
Training Complex

Heat of Love Series
Slow Heat
Alpha Heat
Slow Birth
Bitter Heat
Winter's Heart

'90s Coming of Age Series
Pictures of You
You Are Not Me

Co-Authored with Indra Vaughn
Vespertine
Cowboy Seeks Husband

Co-Authored with Alice Griffiths
The Wake Up Married serial
Will & Patrick's Endless Honeymoon

Gay Fairy Tales
Co-Authored with Keira Andrews
Flight
Levity
Rise

Audiobooks
Leta Blake at Audible

Free Read
Stalking Dreams

Discover more about the author online:
Leta Blake
letablake.com

About the Author

Author of the bestselling book Smoky Mountain Dreams and the fan favorite Training Season, Leta Blake's educational and professional background is in psychology and finance, respectively. However, her passion has always been for writing. She enjoys crafting romance stories and exploring the psyches of made up people. At home in the Southern U.S., Leta works hard at achieving balance between her day job, her writing, and her family.